Pajama Club Mystery:

Something cozy this way comes...

By Maizie Waters

Book One in the Pajama Club Mystery series

Copyright 2020
By Mr. Z. Publications

Contact info
dchampoux@gmail.com
413-575-3411
Or find the Maizie Waters page on Amazon

Part One: What Happened to Monday?

Wanda Beecher heard a noise out back. Or was it from the basement? No. Couldn't be, because what would someone be doing in the basement?

She stood at her baking table with her wooden spoon poised in mid-air, and she waited. Nothing.

It was probably nothing.

She stirred the batter and then poured it into a muffin tin and slid the whole thing into the oven.

She checked the clock: five-thirty in the morning. At five forty-five, that sweet girl Lizzie from across the street would arrive, probably still in her pajamas. She'd apologize for coming into the shop before it officially opens at six, and Wanda would give the answer she always gives: "I don't mind in the least, Sweetheart. You're always welcome here."

Wanda checked the second oven for the triple-chocolate oatmeal cookies she put in earlier - a new item she was baking just to mix things up a little, so to speak.

She took out the cookies and placed them on the counter to cool.

Then she heard another noise. A door closing? Had Lizzie come in earlier than usual?

She looked out the front window, but all she saw was early morning darkness. And all she heard was silence.

"Oh, well," she told herself. "I was right the first time: it's probably nothing."

But she hadn't imagined the noises; she really hadn't. They must have come from somewhere. She walked down the hallway to the rear of her shop and looked out the back door. Near the dumpster, she saw a white van, rusted and mud-spattered.

New neighbors moving into the shop next door? How nice. Something to mix things up a little.

So to speak.

A Night at June's

All day at work, people talk about the plan to meet at five o'clock for cocktails at Saucy June's. You know that place at the mall? It's not my kind of place, to be honest with you. I mean, it's fine. I like the wings. And everyone keeps saying, "Lizzie, you're coming too, right?" - not as a question, but as a statement. So of course I smile and nod. But I don't really get the idea of going out on a Monday no matter *whose* birthday it is. And June's is always so loud and... *mall*-y. You know what I'm saying? Which is fine, really. But it's not the kind of place you can bring a book, let's put it that way. And I'm totally into this mystery I started when I had my coffee-and-muffin early this morning. It's about this girl who finally meets her neighbor in the next apartment, and she turns out to be really nice. But the very next day the woman disappears, and... well, I won't spoil it for you, except to say that it's really good so far.

And, okay, *possibly* one of the other reasons I'm not looking forward to June's is that I know - I can just *feel* - that I'll see Aaron there.

It's a simple intuition, and I know I'm right.

So why? Why do I think I'll see Aaron there, especially given all the reasons he *wouldn't* be there? Like, for one thing, he doesn't work in our division anymore. And his new office isn't anywhere near the mall. And he could certainly be on a business trip, since it's conference season for the textile industry (fun fact!). And for that matter, he's really not much of a drinker to begin with. He doesn't need cocktails because he gets drunk on people. Talking to them. Being around them. Winning them over and making friends. And that's why he'll go to June's tonight, and it's also why he has a bright future at TechTile Incorporated: our office is always having parties, luncheons, parties, dinner-meetings, parties, conferences...

and did I mention the parties?

I know that someone will invite him. I mean, of course - right? What's a party without Aaron?

And now that he's on my mind, I see reminders of him everywhere: his travel mug in the cupboard of the breakroom. His name as co-author of a report we wrote together. His smiling face sticking out of a potato sack in a photo from the team-building day mini-Olympics.

And to top it off, I hear the song. Our song.

We have a new speaker system in the office, and to brighten the mood with background music, Jannelle put on a streaming station called 'Soft Rock through the Years.'

And wouldn't you know that of all the soft rock songs throughout all the years, the one that comes on at the very moment Jannelle flips the switch is "Giving You the Best that I've Got." Anita Baker, 1988.

Ugh.

I hate that song.

I mean, I *used* to like the song. Not all that long ago, you could even say I loved it. I'd sing it while I rode my bike to buy groceries for stay-in dates with Aaron. And I sang it as I walked through the aisles of the wine and cheese shop, looking at the different labels, even though I always ended up getting the same bottle of Malbec, and the same wedge of smoked Gouda.

Our Malbec. *Our* cheese. *Our* stay-in date.

Our song.

When I used to hear it I'd think of those two things: Malbec and smoked Gouda - which, by the way, go really good together.

Just like Aaron and I used to go good together.

Used to.

But now when the song comes on, I just hear the line: *I bet everything on my wedding ring*. It's a triumphant declaration: she's all in. No hesitation, no turning back. Beautiful, right?

Yeah, sure. But it's just a song, though. It's not real life.

Because in real life, I bet everything on red: hearts, roses, a ruby ring. And the roulette wheel of love came up black.

Saucy June's.

It's soup night. Sounds good, right? Nice and cozy?

The idea is great. But the soup itself? Not so good. It's a potato soup with, as far as I can tell, a cheese base. It's a bowl of cheese, that's what it is. Which, okay, cheese is good. But no. As in… *no*.

Wait, have I become a cheese snob all the sudden? First I'm going on about smoked Gouda, and now this?

Anyway.

Whatever else I think about the place, I have to give June's credit for their wings, because these are *really* good. And I've been trying for, like, two years now to figure out how they make the sauce.

So I continue my culinary investigation. Sitting at one of the back tables, I take a spoonful of sauce from the wings and spread it out on the white part of my plate. I lean way down to examine it closely. Are those bits of spices I'm seeing? Grains of cocoa? A cocoa sauce would be good, like a Mexican molé kind of thing. I don't quite taste cocoa, though.

After multiple trials and experimentations, my best guess is that the sauce is made from orange rind, cayenne pepper, and caramel.

And I know you're thinking, *"Caramel?"* But really, you should taste these and tell me what you think is in them, because they are beyond over-the-top good and I would love to figure out the recipe.

Anyway, I'm spreading the sauce around the plate with the edge of a fork to really thin it out and get a sense of its density, and I hear a voice.

"What are you doing, reading tea leaves?"

I look up. It's my sister, dropping by on her way home from work.

"Hi, Fi," I say, glad to see her - but also cringing a little.

You see, she has that look of affectionate pity that only an older sister can have. And I don't get it. Why should she pity me? Just because I'm sitting in the back of the room, alone at a two-top, with my face two inches from my plate?

She's actually about to tell me why she pities me. But then the Media table shouts, pretty much in unison, "Fiona!"

Yes, they give her this glorious greeting, even though she doesn't work at TechTile. She doesn't even work in the same business we do. She's a forensic psychologist, and we are a textile brokerage firm. These are not even remotely similar lines of work. But she's dropped in on enough of these work party things (usually to rescue me, if I'm honest) that she now gets a bigger welcome than I do.

And in case you were wondering, no. No one shouted my name when I walked in here. But, I mean, I wouldn't *want* a whole table of people to shout my name, in public, no matter how friendly they intend it to be. If that did happen, I'd probably be all, like, "What? What did I do?" - thinking that I'd done something wrong.

Not Fi, though. She just smiles and waves at them.

"You getting a drink?" she says to me.

"Why? Can you stay a while?"

She checks her watch. "I have, get this, two whole hours!"

"Wow - that's, like, a week's vacation in parent-years. How'd you arrange that?"

"Joe signed the girls up for swim lessons at the Y. It's perfect. They shower afterwards, so we skip the nightly bath entirely. And for the first time since we had kids, I feel this rush of freedom on Monday nights, when I can do whatever I want until eight o'clock."

"Fiona unleashed!" I say. "Well, I hate to disappoint you, but I probably won't have a drink. But you go ahead. Their pinot isn't bad. Sounds like you want one."

"I don't think I do want a drink, actually. It's more like I feel like I should get one, just because I can."

"Alright, then try these wings instead."

She takes a bite. "Whoa, that is good."

And before I can ask her what she thinks about the sauce, someone else shouts "Fiona!" as they walk by our table. I don't even see who it is this time. But they kind of, sort of, wave at me too as they pass, which is good. Having Fi at my table always works out well, because I get to look like I'm being social without having to actually *be* social. Being known as 'Fi's younger sister' has done me a lot of good in my life. And it does me good now too, because Jannelle even comes over and sits with us. She likes Fi, and that rubs off on me, I think. The Office Manager is a good person to have on your side.

And check this out: now that my sister's here with me, I actually say some things.

Like, I speak! As in, I contribute to the conversation!

For example, Fiona says, "I still can't decide what kind of cake to make for Emmy's birthday. What do you think? What's the best cake you've ever had?"

And Jannelle says, "I've got a great funnel cake recipe. It makes a huge, glorious mess that kids just love."

So I say - get this - "Yeah, funnel cakes are good."

And Jannelle looks up at me, startled, like she's pleasantly surprised to learn that I can actually talk at all about anything besides quarterly reports. And even with those, I talk about them as little as possible. I.e., quarterly.

When she recovers herself, Jannelle says, "Yes, they are good, aren't they?"

Then she smiles and resumes talking to Fi. But from that point on, she actually glances over at me once in a while.

So it worked! I said something, and someone else responded.

I am part of the conversation.

And yes, it tells you something about me that the last sentence is in italics, or that I would even remark on any of this at all.

I mean, okay, yes - I am exaggerating just a little bit about how reserved and withdrawn I can be at times.

But it's definitely true that the whole evening is a challenge for me, especially since I could have just gone home and turned on a mystery movie - which, oh my gosh, there's a *really* good one on cable tonight that I'm totally going to watch the next time they air it.

But instead, I'm out on the town. Doing things. Challenging myself. Seeing people, and actually talking to them.

The evening is going well, is my point. It really is.

And now, on cue... wait for it...

Aaron walks in.

Yes, Aaron.

And does he look good?

Yes. He looks very good. No surprise there, of course. He pretty much always looks good. I don't think I've never seen a collar as crisp as the one he has on now - certainly not at the end of a work-day. His suit is charcoal pinstripe, and his shirt is an eggshell blue cotton blend with a soft sheen to it. And... wow. I mean, I generally prefer a plaid flannel shirt, personally, but there's no denying he can pull off this professional look. Relaxed yet confident. You could call it 'formal-business-casual' or something like that - which isn't even a thing, but it should be. They could name it after Aaron. The Aaron Look.

"And is he accompanied by anyone?" you ask.

Why yes, he is.

In fact, he's brought his new girlfriend Ashley. And she's wearing... wait for it...

A black. Lycra. Cocktail dress.

"A black cocktail dress on a *Monday*?" you ask.

Yes, on a Monday, I answer.

"Is the dress tight?" you ask.

Don't ask.

Just picture yoga pants as a whole dress. Or half of a dress, to be completely accurate.

So I'm sitting here, not staring at Aaron and Ashley -

which is to say, I'm totally staring at them, if you know what I mean - when I feel a gentle poke in my ribs. It's Fiona, giving me a 'be strong, girl' look.

And I think, "Okay, okay. You're right, Fi. I'll be strong. And as long as he doesn't approach me, I'll be fine."

So what do you think happens?

He approaches me.

"Eliza!" he says. He always uses my full name - which on the one hand is nice because it's respectful. But on the other hand, it kind of sounds like my uncle Liam at Christmas asking me things like, "And how are you getting on in school these days, young lady?" - even though I graduated from high school ten years ago and college six years ago.

And just like Uncle Liam, Aaron booms my name so loud that I can't pretend I don't hear it.

So I smile at him. I mean, not *at* him, because I can't actually bring myself to make eye contact. And it's not actually a smile, either. I just kind of do something with my mouth that I think is probably smiley. And just to bring home the point, I squint my eyes in that 'eye-smile' thing some people do.

But obviously none of this works because Jannelle looked at me, like, 'Are you *okay*?'

Yes - I'm okay.

I mean, I'm not okay. But I'm *okay*. If you know what I mean.

"Eliza, I didn't know if you'd be here tonight," Aaron says. "But I'm so glad you've come. I've really been hoping to introduce you to Ashley."

Yes. You're hearing it right. He's really hoping to introduce me to his new girlfriend - who, *hello*, I already know her because she works at TechTile! Or at least I know *of* her. She's on the travel team with Aaron, so I don't see her much, but I still had to witness their courtship from afar. I can even pinpoint the moment it began at the company softball game last fall. Ashely came up to bat with two runners on base.

Petite, girly Ashley. And when all the outfielders moved in, thinking that she couldn't hit the ball past the pitcher's mound, she promptly hit a line drive over their heads for a double. The two runners score, and the game swings our way.

Aaron was one of those two base runners, and I remember the look on his face when he crossed home plate and then spun around to watch Ashely make it safe into second.

He was smiling, of course.

He talked to her after the game. They went out for a drink. And they've been together since.

And the thing you have to understand about Aaron is that it probably sounds like he's rubbing it in, flaunting the fact that he's with someone new. But he isn't. He really is glad to see me, and he really does want me to meet Ashley. And of course he thinks I'm just dying to meet her.

Right? Because doesn't every woman want to meet her ex's new girlfriend?

And I actually hope - and I know this isn't my best self talking - but I actually hope she'll turn out to be a jerk, so that I can say (in my head, of course - not out loud), "Good for you, Aaron. Have fun with your new jerk girlfriend who makes you miserable."

But no. She's not a jerk. In fact, she smiles at me and compliments me on my keychain - this woolen lanyard that I knitted and then felted.

"That's so neat," she says. "I wouldn't know how to begin to do that, but you're so handy. Aaron's always telling me about these little things you make."

She seems genuinely impressed, and if we weren't at a restaurant, I might even show her how to make one, because they're not that hard. And, as I said, she's actually kind of, you know, nice.

But even though she's nice, I still can't get over the fact that she's not... *me*.

Do you know what I'm saying?

For example, she's totally 'dressed to impress,' whereas

my first criteria for clothing is, 'Could I sleep in this if I had to?' She's bright and perky at six o'clock, just getting started on what will undoubtedly be a long evening, whereas I'm wondering how much longer I need to stay here in order to get credit for going to a work event.

But... I don't know. I guess it's kind of good that she's not the same as me. Because if Aaron dumped me and then found someone else who was just like me, I'd think, 'What does *she* offer that I don't?'

And so, having thoroughly overthought the situation as usual, I say something nice to Ashley about her earrings - which are these simple, classy silver hoops. And she starts telling the story of how Aaron bought them for her on their last conference trip together. The hotel had a little gift shop, and she kept admiring the earrings each time she passed the window. So finally Aaron slipped down there during a break between seminars, and he bought them for her as a surprise. And isn't that so sweet?

Don't I think that's just so totally sweet?

"Yeah, sure," I say.

But what I really think is... ugh. I want nothing more than to retreat to the back of the room. But I can't do that for two reasons. One is that I'm stuck right in the middle of the conversation, and as freaky as I am, I haven't taken to just leaving conversations mid-sentence. Not yet, anyway. And two is that I can't retreat to the back of the room because I'm already *in* the back of the room where I always sit.

But all of this is interrupted anyway when one of June's kitchen workers enters from the service door right near us carrying a big cake, and everyone starts singing "Happy Birthday" to Sarah from Media, the guest of honor. And our table, which had been in the back of the room, is all the sudden in what's become the new front of the room, with all the attention coming this way. Jannelle conducts the song like the maestro of a symphony, and Danny from Sales does his falsetto thing, and everyone is singing and crowding in our direction.

So with all this going on, it's not hard for me to just kind of melt out of the way as the group converges around Sarah. When Fi sees what I'm doing, she rolls her eyes at me. But I grab her sleeve, and she melts with me. And before long, we're in the back of the room again - the new back. By this time they've lowered the lights to make the candles look better, which gives everything a sepia look to it, like an old movie or a scene from a mystery novel.

And that makes me think about home. My apartment.

Where I like to watch old movies and read mystery novels.

So I turn to Fiona and I say, "I'm leaving."

"What? No - you can't leave," she says, because she's all about strength, Fiona is. "You can't run from your problems."

I agree. You can't. But I'm not running from my problems. I'm running *towards* my couch. I'm running *towards* watching an old movie, huddled under SuperFuzz - which, by the way, you *do* have a name for your sofa-blanket, right? Everyone does.

I mean… Right?

And the thing is, when I mention the couch and my blanket and the movie, Fi's eyes widen just a little bit - such a little bit that if I didn't know her as well as I do, I wouldn't notice it.

But I do notice it. And I know what it means: she wants to come too.

So Fi and I caravan home from Saucy June's, driving out of the mall parking lot, down busy Route 5 and then out Old County Road - eventually making our way to Teabridge Village, and finally my apartment. I climb into some cozy fleece pj's, and I make some chamomile tea.

It's a nice moment to collect our heads and settle in after the whirlwind of Saucy June's. Well, for me it's a whirlwind. For other people it's fun, I'm sure. Extroverted people, like Fi. And that makes me feel bad for dragging her out of there.

"I'm sorry I made you not have a good time on your one night out," I tell her.

She tries to give me a stern glance, but she can't hold it. "You didn't make me not have a good time," she says. "To be honest with you. Lizzie, I don't think you could. You are the sanest and the craziest girl I know - both at the same time, somehow."

I give her a hug. She hugs me back.

"Actually," she says, "if you had dragged me out of there before the wings came out, you would have spoiled the evening. But you didn't do that. And my gosh, those are good. What's in the sauce, anyway? Butterscotch?"

"Interesting idea," I say. "Caramel is my best guess so far. But I like your thinking, because it's definitely something sweet and buttery. We should experiment sometime."

She smiles. "That would be fun. And tasty, if we figured out the recipe."

"I think it would be tasty even if we didn't figure it out," I say, and she laughs. Then I ask her, "Can you stay for a movie?"

"Ooh. I don't know. Joe's had the kids since school let out. Let me see how they're doing."

She video-calls her husband.

"Painting the town red, I see," Joe says, leaning toward the screen, noticing us all wrapped up in SuperFuzz.

"Painting it sepia, according to Lizzie," Fi says. "Where are the kids? Can I say goodnight?"

"Emmy's in the bath, and Grace is, I *think*, finally getting on her pajamas. But she can hear me talking to you, so I'm sure she'll be out soon."

"I'm glad that they're settling in, because I want to ask you something."

"Let me guess," Joe says. "You and Lizzie want to watch a movie."

"You know us too well," Fi says. "Can I stay?"

At that very moment, Grace walks into the frame, tangled

up in her pajama shirt. I think she's put her arm in the neck-hole. But, wow, it's so tangled, you can't even tell. And the more Joe tries to help her, the worse it gets.

When they've finally gotten it sorted out, Joe looks exhausted. He turns to the phone. "Um… How about half a movie?"

"Deal," Fiona says. And that actually is a perfect deal, because I usually fall asleep halfway through movies anyway. Then I save the other half for the next time Fi comes over.

"Before you hang up, Emmy wants to know if she can say 'hi,'" Joe says.

On cue, Emily crowds into the picture. She's obviously come straight from the bathtub. As in *straight* from the bathtub without even grabbing a towel, never mind using one.

"Hi Mom! Hi Aunt Lizzie!" she squeals.

"Hi, Sweetie," I say. "How are you doing?"

"Um… I'm really wet."

"I can see that," I say. "You're also shivering."

"Uh-huh."

"So…" I say. "Do you think you should maybe dry off?"

"Good idea," Emmy says, as though the idea had never occurred to her and never would have. Then she disappears, hopefully to find a towel, but more likely to get distracted by the names of the different countries on their plastic map-of-the-world shower curtain.

Fi leans toward me. "Kids can be so smart sometimes, but other times…"

I nod, to save her from having to finish the sentence.

We say goodnight to the girls and then to Joe, thanking him profusely for the extra time he's granted us.

"Alright," Fi says, shoving her phone deep into her pocket. "Let the revelry begin."

"Yes!" I say. "Okay, first thing: come to the window with me."

We walk over to the double-window in the front of the apartment, overlooking Cottage Street. I push aside the white curtains that I love because they're knitted in a pattern of diamonds and flowery loops that make me feel like I live in an English country village. Which I almost do, really, because I live in New England - which has 'England' right in the name - and Teabridge is a village. Two facts of which I am inordinately proud.

We look out on that village.

"I have a new tradition," I tell Fi. "Before I settle in for the night, I like to say goodnight to everything."

"You mean like *Goodnight Moon*?"

"Very much like *Goodnight Moon*," I say. "The Teabridge edition. I go from biggest to smallest. First I say, 'Goodnight stars.' Then I say, 'Goodnight moon.' Then 'Goodnight clouds,' if there are any. Then I come down to earth, and I say, 'Goodnight Edicom mountain range. Goodnight Fir Tree Hill.' And then I say goodnight to the stores across the street, from right to left: 'Goodnight, Tile and Flooring store. Goodnight Muffins. Goodnight empty storefront. Goodnight bank. Good night financial advisor thingy-place, whatever it is - which I should probably know exactly what it is, now that I'm mostly, kind of, an adult. Goodnight alley to the back parking lot. Goodnight convenience store on the other side of the alley. Goodnight curve in the road that makes it so I can't see anything else.'"

"Gosh, you are thorough," Fi says.

"Wait. I'm not done yet," I say. "Then I come inside: Goodnight curtains. Goodnight easy chair. Good night lights."

I turn off the lights, just as I say goodnight to them. Then I take a nice, deep, end of the day breath.

"Alright, so now you're done?" Fi says.

"Now I'm done."

"Then next is… hello movie?"

"Yes," I say, laughing. "Hello, movie."

We sit back down on the couch together, pulling SuperFuzz over us, and I grab Multiplex - which is what I call my tablet. And at this point I'm not even going to ask if you have a name for your tablet that you watch movies on, because of course you do. Everyone does, right?

"What's on the bill tonight?" Fi says.

"Well, I'm thinking *The Lady Vanishes* - which we haven't seen in, like, forever..."

"The Hitchcock movie?"

"Of course."

"We watched that together eight months ago," she says.

"Yeah, that's what I said: forever."

We settle in and get all the way to the part where Iris, the Margaret Lockwood character, falls asleep. And that's when (spoiler alert!) her friend Miss Froy vanishes. And that's when, yes, I fall asleep, too. Which is kind of cool in its own way, when what happens in a movie is exactly what happens in real life.

When I wake up in the darkness of eleven-thirty at night, Fiona is long gone home to her husband and girls, and Multiplex is sitting on the coffee table, neatly folded back into its case.

I go into my room and climb into my bed. I sink into the mattress and sleep blissfully for another seven hours, deep under the cover of The Big Fluff.

Yes, I have a name for my double-thick down comforter.

But I do not have a name for my bed - which you think I would, given how well it treats me.

Part Two: Tuesday Never Comes

Wanda felt... uneasy. Or was it 'concerned'? Maybe. But if so, what about? If you're concerned, you have to be concerned <u>about</u> something, don't you?

Some guys were moving into the empty shop next door, that's true. But so what? She was glad. No reason for concern there.

Still, it was strange that they hadn't stopped in to introduce themselves for two mornings in a row now, even though you'd think they would - especially this early when they were clearly the only ones up. Besides Lizzie from across the street, of course.

There were three men: two in their early thirties, and a young one - still a teenager. He was different from the others. When she was bringing her cardboard recycling back to the dumpster, he paused like he wanted to say hello and introduce himself after all. But one of the others checked him with a hard look.

Oh well, she thought. That could mean anything.

Live and let live, and assume the best.

After all, when she first heard them arrive yesterday, she wondered if something sketchy was going on. But in the end, nothing came of it. At least nothing she'd seen.

If they didn't introduce themselves today, then she'd approach them. Yes. That was a good idea.

Unless it wasn't.

Muffin for One

When I wake up, I make myself a mocha. Then I pull my easy chair up close to the double-window in the living room, overlooking Teabridge Village square, and I settle in to read *Tea for One*, the mystery book I'm currently on. I end up finishing it, actually. It's a takeoff on *The Lady Vanishes*, which is probably why I wanted to watch that movie last night. This young woman lives in an apartment in the city, and she has this elderly neighbor who's really reclusive to the point where, even after living in the building for two years, the young woman has never run into the neighbor even once.

Then one day she *does* run into her. And they have a nice conversation. And they plan to have tea together the following day.

But the neighbor doesn't show up for tea - surprise, surprise. So the young woman starts thinking something's happened to her. But whenever she tries to tell anyone this, they're all, like, *What old woman are you talking about?* Because even though everyone always heard that an old woman lived in the apartment, no one else had ever actually seen her. And so they doubt the whole story, saying things like, "Didn't you have a cold this week that you needed to take cough medicine for?" like the whole thing was just a hazy diphenhydramine-induced dream.

And at the end of each chapter, I peek through the curtains to see if the light in Wanda's muffin shop has come on yet. Then I go back to reading. And before I know it, I finish the whole book, and you're not going to believe it, but...

Wait. I said I wasn't going to spoil the ending, so I won't.

I close the book and look down, and there it is, right on cue: the light in Wanda's shop comes on at this very moment. It's almost like Wanda waited for me to get to the end of the book before she started her day.

So I get up and I go down to her shop, dressed just as I am. Yes, out in public wearing my pajamas, because why not? And I mean, I'm the furthest thing from an exhibitionist, obviously, but I know Wanda wouldn't care, and my big wool coat covers nearly every inch of me.

For that matter, my pajama shirt *kind of* looks like a blouse - from a distance, anyway. It's got purple wisterias on a white background in a pattern so tight that it's basically purple. And if you saw just the collar peeking out of a coat, wouldn't you think I was wearing a nice blouse?

As far as the pants go - well, they actually do look like pajama bottoms. There's no getting around that. They're all baggy-fleecy, with a thick-stitched hem at the cuffs. But I still didn't want to change them, because my plan is to go get a muffin and then snuggle right back into the easy chair by the window and pick my next mystery to read. And mystery novels are always good, but don't they feel just a little bit better when you're in your pajamas?

Doesn't pretty much everything feel better when you're in your pajamas?

So. I don't change them.

And when I step out of my apartment door into the hallway, I feel like I'm in a suspense movie: a young woman must sneak across enemy lines to secure a muffin. That's the MacGuffin. Have you heard of that movie term? It's a Hitchcock thing. The MacGuffin is the goal or the object that keeps the plot moving, like some secret plans that the heroine has to sneak out of a foreign country, which sets her out on a long, elaborate journey where she meets a man. And they clash and don't like each other and are totally not right for each other, but of course throughout the movie they stick together and save each other and have ten or twelve interrupted kisses until they finally deliver the secret plans and realize that they really are quite right for each other after all.

Music swells. Uninterrupted kiss. Roll credits.

So there it is. In the suspense movie of my life, the MacGuffin is a muffin. And nothing will stop me from achieving it. Not wind nor rain nor shyness about wearing pajamas in public.

I walk down the creakle-stairs (this is a *really* old building) past the mailboxes in the dusty little foyer and then out the front door.

My destination: the row of buildings across the street, just thirty-five feet away.

But I imagine that the street is a heath and I am crossing it in a storm. I look both ways to check for rogues on wild dark horses, and then I take a deep breath and forge ahead as a bitter rush of freezing wind permeates my jacket and my pajamas, and then finally it permeates *me*. I pull my collar tighter around me and just keep moving until I finally reach the front of Wanda's bakery. I grasp the cold brass doorknob, but I barely feel it because the wind has numbed my fingers. Still, I press the lever and slip through the door.

The air inside is thick and warm, infused with yeast, sugar, and baked blueberries. It's like I'm stepping *into* a muffin.

I pass the seating area, which is about the size of a small living room with a couch and a coffee table in the middle, three round cafe tables lining the window, and an easy chair next to them.

And if this arrangement of furniture sounds so familiar that you're thinking, 'Lizzie, did you set up your own living room to be just like the muffin shop?' - well, you might, *possibly*, be right.

I walk past all that to the counter along the side. And at this very moment, Wanda comes out from the kitchen area. Smudges of white flour on her dark brown skin make her look like an artist working in pastels. She's carrying a plate of chocolate-covered triple-chocolate oatmeal cookies, a recipe she just invented yesterday which is, like, *whoa*.

"Good morning, Sweetie," she says, and she keeps moving - arranging trays, turning on the coffee maker. The shop isn't technically open yet, so she hasn't booted up the register. I could just take a muffin from the pan and leave the money on the counter, which I've done a bunch of times, and she doesn't mind it at all. But I kind of want to just stay here, because I enjoy watching her work.

You see, she's busy, but she's not rushing as she lays the cookies out on the tray and arranges the signs in the display case.

She doesn't even notice my pajamas. Or if she does, she doesn't care, of course. She's obviously much more interested in her work than in my clothes. And actually, something else seems to have her attention as well, though I can't tell what it is - except that at one point she pauses like she'd heard a noise. And she actually looks troubled, which I have to say gives me a little jolt of anxiety. Wanda is the most serene person I know, and if she's bothered by something, it must be pretty big. So we listen for a moment but don't hear anything, and she resumes working in her usual calm, peaceful way. She's Wanda again, and I'm glad. In fact, 'being Wanda' is exactly what I want to ask her about.

"Can I ask you something?" I say. "How is it that you're able to like your job so much?"

"Don't you like yours?" she says, obviously sensing the real reason for my question. "Seems like a fine job for a young woman to have."

She's right. It is a fine job. I should be grateful to have it, and I am. But I don't approach it the way Wanda approaches her work, that's for sure.

Wanda does her work the way I get ready to watch a movie or read on the couch. I just ask myself, "What can I do to make this situation so much nicer?" And then I do whatever I come up with. Like, I might get an extra blanket or a knitted hat so I can be extra cozy. Or I might make some bread to go with my tea. Or who knows what I'll think of next? When I'm getting ready like that, I don't worry about deadlines or people's impressions or anything like that. I'm just quietly thrilled as I do all these happy things to make a good time even better.

And that's how Wanda is, at least here. I don't know her well enough to say how she lives the rest of her life. But it can't be much different, because she has such a naturally relaxed way about her, smiling after every step in the process of setting up her shop, like she's proud of each small accomplishment and looking forward to the next one.

Then Wanda asks me a question that catches me off guard so much that I don't even really notice it at first. She's arranging plates in the display case, still not actually looking at me, and she says, "Do you know what you want, Sweetheart?"

And I pretty much always get a blueberry muffin when she has them available, so I pick up one of those with a piece of wax paper - and, what the heck, a chocolate-covered triple-chocolate oatmeal cookie for later - and I hand her the money.

And finally she does make eye contact with me. "Always so nice to see you," she says. "My early morning friend."

And that's the sweetest, nicest thing she could possibly say to me at this moment. My heart fills up and I want to hug her. Or at least to tell her how nice it is to see her, too.

But then she gets distracted again, like she's heard another noise, maybe. She heads off, down to the storeroom in her basement or wherever that door leads to. And so I leave.

I walk across the street and back up to my apartment, and I sit in the easy chair up near the front window, where I like to watch the village wake up.

I see an old sedan pull up to the front of the convenience store, delivering a stack of papers to Sheila, the owner of the store. She strolls out, picks up the stack, cuts the cord, and lays the papers out on the stand near the front window.

Then, after a pause, the Honor Court van rolls up, carrying men from the recovery shelter in Leighton. They're here to pick up the trash from the bins. It's a transitional job that gets them back into the swing of work, and they're good at it - sweeping through in only a few minutes.

Then after another pause, I see a jogger go by. I see a businesswoman getting early coffee from the convenience store. I see the bank supervisor show up early.

You can say Teabridge is quiet, but things are happening. People are coming and going. Wanda is baking away in the back of her shop. Sheila is stocking shelves. And I am up here, perched. Watching.

I settle in with my muffin and mocha. And yes, the fact that both words begin with 'M' does make them seem better together, somehow.

I take a breath.

I take a sip.

I eat a piece of blueberry muffin. Just a piece, though. I don't pick up the whole muffin and take a bite. Do you do that? I don't. I break off pieces and eat them one at a time. I just like it better this way, like each piece is a little muffin - so instead of eating one whole muffin, I eat, like, twenty of them. Or more? I don't know how many bites I take, but these muffins are big, and I like to make them last.

I lean back in the chair. Yes, I will get up soon, and I'll get ready for the day. And I'll go into work at TechTile, and I'll do my job, and it will all be good and fine.

But just one more minute here.

I stare at my bookshelf, thinking about what my next book will be now that I've finished *Tea for One*. I've read all the books on my shelf, though. Except... wait. One of the spines looks unfamiliar. I lean forward and pull it out. It's a mystery novel I don't remember buying. It must be from the library's sale-shelf, because it has a catalogue sticker on the binding. I slide it out and take a look.

It's called *The Wayward Daughter*, and the back cover says that it's about this woman who comes back to town when her mother dies, only to find these strange things in the will that don't make sense to her. And she starts to think these weird little details are coded messages from her mother that she missed the first time she saw them.

And as I read this book description, a cold feeling comes over my chest. Does that ever happen to you when you're reading, where something that happens in the book applies to your life so completely that you have to just stop reading and take it in?

Well, that happens to me now. I have the feeling that something big just passed by me, and I almost missed it - just like the woman in the book almost missed the clues that her mother was giving her.

You see, just a few minutes ago, down in the muffin shop, Wanda asked me if I knew what I wanted. And I just immediately assumed she meant, 'Do you want a blueberry muffin or a cranberry muffin?'

But the reason I'm now a little stunned is because...

Was she asking me *more* than just what kind of muffin I wanted?

I'm sitting here, stunned, thinking about it.

Do you know what you want?

It's such a simple question, but at the same time it's so... big. It could mean so many things.

Like the question could mean, 'Do you know what you want for your career?' Wanda and I had been talking about my job, so maybe that's what she meant. And the truth is, I'm a little stuck at work. I mean, my job is secure because I do whatever they ask me to do, and I do it well enough. But I know they like innovation. They like outside-the-box thinking. And, if I'm honest, I like boxes. I like them so much that if I was ever reincarnated as an animal, I'd be a cat, for sure.

Wanda's question could also mean, 'Do you know what you want for your social life?' And the truth is, I kind of don't have that much of a social life right now. I mean, I have Fi, and that's great. And Fi has me, too, which is great as well. But she also has her kids, and she has Joe, and she has friends from work, and she has friends just because they're friends, and...

well, you get the idea.

Or the question could mean, 'Do you know what you want for a relationship?' And I'm pretty stuck there, too. And what I'm stuck on is… wait for it… Aaron.

That might, possibly, *not* be a surprise to you.

But what *could* be a surprise to you, given how raw the whole thing feels to me, is that we broke up over a year ago.

Yes, more than a whole year.

And, to be clear, the relationship is done for me. I don't want to be with Aaron anymore, and I'm really okay with that fact that he doesn't want to be with me. We liked each other. We cared for each other. But we weren't right for each other.

So if all that's true, why haven't I moved on?

The memories. That's why.

We used to go for hikes in these quiet woods along the Edicom River, and then we'd come back here to Teabridge and sit in Wanda's for a snack, or we'd bring it up here to the apartment and get cozy on the couch. And in the winter, I got him to watch old movies. And he even got me to go out to a restaurant in Leighton sometimes, and I'd feel like a little kid going out to eat in the big city. Then we'd come home here and find out if Charlie in *Shadow of a Doubt* ever figures out what her uncle Joseph Cotton is up to. I mean, I knew the answer because I've seen the movie six times, obviously. But it's still fun every time, especially when I can share it with someone new, like Aaron.

Actually, all that happened much more than a year ago, because we didn't do much of any of those things towards the end. You know how sometimes in the last few months of a relationship, you're a couple in name only, because you're already going your separate ways? The breakup is really just when both of you finally realize it

It was no one's fault, really. It's just how things go sometimes. No promises were broken, and we were never even formally engaged. I know I said all that earlier about the wedding ring in the Anita Baker song. But that was just talk, because we didn't get that far. Just, you know, in my mind, we got that far...

Then he got a promotion. He became 'the conference guy,' which means lots of traveling. Out and about. Hotels and meet-and-greets and drinks after meetings. Shaking hands and handing out his business card. And now he's with Ashley, and she loves all that stuff, apparently. She's, like, twenty-three or something, if that. A younger woman.

I'm only twenty-eight. How can I be old enough for there to be a 'younger woman'?

But... whatever. It's fine.

They certainly seemed happy enough last night, so good for them. I guess he got what he wanted: someone who likes that same life he does. Dressing up and socializing and staying out late, party to party.

I had that life once. Or a glimpse of it, anyway. And if I'd just kept up with Aaron, I'd still have it.

And all that makes me sad.

It makes me pull my blanket over myself even more snugly, as I sink deeper into my easy chair in my comfortable pajamas. It makes me want to cover my whole head with the blanket and just stay here. I'll read and I'll eat comfort food treats and peak out through the blanket and watch the little village of Teabridge slowly wake up around me.

That's it. I'm not getting dressed again - *ever*.

I'm staying in my pajamas.

Yup.

I'm staying right here like this, and I'm not moving.

And, yes, I am aware that if my sister Fi saw me right now, she'd say, "Lizzie - really, now. You need to get real. Wrapping yourself in a blanket and chain-reading mystery novels all day long? You're being ridiculous."

The problem, of course, is that I don't feel ridiculous. In fact, I feel pretty good.

And if Fi heard me say *that*, she'd say, "Lizzie, you can't live in a cocoon, you know. You should get out there and face life."

And okay, fine. She's probably right.

But I don't want to face life. I want to stay here, just exactly like this.

And you know what? I don't have to do what my older sister tells me to do, no matter how grown up and responsible she is. I'm twenty-eight years old, and I can make my own decisions.

So that's it. I've made my own decision: from now on, I'm staying in my pajamas.

Is this what you meant, Wanda, when you asked me what I wanted? Is this what you were trying to get me to figure out?

I lean forward in my chair. I peek out from under the blanket. And I look down at the muffin shop, to see if Wanda is there to give me an answer.

Then I hear a noise.

Small Surprises

A clanging. Or a banging. Or a jostling of things. I don't know.

I lean further forward and push the lace curtain aside with my nose, sticking my face through the space before the curtain falls back again.

Wanda *is* down there, standing in the doorway of her shop. She must be the one who made the noise, probably when she officially opened up her shop for the day. She pauses as she lingers for a moment. She takes a breath and looks up and down the street, which is empty and quiet at the moment. Then she turns and goes back inside.

Seeing her again makes me want to ask her what she meant earlier when she said, "Do you know what you want?" It was just a simple question, but it's still kind of lingering for me. And she's so sweet to talk to. So you know what? I'll go talk to her. I'll get ready for work, and I'll stop in again on my way down to my car.

So I get dressed - begrudgingly, but I do it. I change out of my wisteria flannels and into some work slacks and a smart white button-down shirt.

I check myself in the full-length mirror on the back of my closet door, and I'm surprised because I look kind of… sharp. I mean, honestly, it's more accurate to say that I look almost-sharp. But for me, almost-sharp *is* sharp, if you know what I mean. And if I added some pearls and a colorful nylon scarf, I'd actually look professional. Executive-y, even.

Instead, I pull on an oversized oatmeal-colored Aran wool sweater with sleeves that dangle past my wrists, covering half of my hands.

And now I just look like 'me' again. That's okay. I'm okay with the fact that I'll never be an executive. At least not while I still use words like 'executive-y.'

I put my lunch together: a peanut butter and banana sandwich on oatmeal bread that I made in my bread machine. The loaf came out lopsided, as usual, and I make my sandwich with an end piece that has valleys and ridges like a topographical map of Edicom County. I rotate the bread so that it slopes up to the low mountain range in the North. The crease that runs diagonally down from right to left becomes the Edicom River. A depression in the lower right left-hand corner becomes Teabridge Village. I put my finger right where my apartment would be. Just to say, "This is me. I am here."

Then I wrap the sandwich because it's too big and weirdly-shaped to fit in a regular fold-over sandwich bag - at least not without smooshing it in there, which I obviously don't want to do.

I put an apple and some baby carrots into my bag. And a cheese stick and four wheat crackers for a snack to have with my tea in the afternoon.

Then I wrap up the chocolate-covered triple-chocolate oatmeal cookie I got at Wanda's this morning, which is a special treat, obviously. I put it in the inside pouch of my lunch bag, and I close my eyes to forget that it's there so that when I open the bag later and eat everything else, I'll look inside the pouch and find it, and it will be like a surprise.

I walk downstairs to the street. It's the Teabridge version of rush hour, which is to say a car passes every five or ten seconds, maybe. Then silence. Then, eventually, another car. While I'm at work, things will actually get a little busier with foot traffic from people shopping on Bank Row, which is the name for the line of shop-fronts that make up the big, continuous building across the street, containing the Tile-and-Flooring shop, Wanda's, the empty place, the bank, and finally the financial office.

Wanda's is, in fact, officially open now, and the rest of the shops will open in the next half hour. Soon people will come and go. I mean, no one will come and go from the empty storefront, obviously. But from the other places, they will.

I cross the street, and halfway over, I remember that two hours ago, in the early morning, I pretended that this was a windy heath. But it's no longer dark and windy enough to be a heath. Now it's just a street.

I should turn it into something, though, because who wants to cross just a street?

So you know what it is now? It's a meadow. Yes, a sunny, breezy mountain meadow with a stream running through it right along the far curb. When I get to the edge, I step over the invisible stream.

I walk up to the front door of the muffin shop, and I step inside. A few of the regulars are sitting in the lounge area, sipping coffee and reading the newspaper.

Wanda isn't behind the counter, though. And she's not back in the kitchen, either - at least not the part of the kitchen I can see from out here.

"Wanda?" I say. And I wait.

No answer.

I call out again, louder. "Wanda?"

Still no answer.

I look at one of the regular customers, but he just shrugs and says, "Saw her a few minutes ago."

"How many minutes is 'a few'?"

He shrugs again. "Ten?"

"Thanks," I say.

I lean over the rear counter to try to see more of the kitchen area. But she doesn't seem to be there. I look at my watch. Unfortunately, I have to get to work soon - otherwise I'd wait.

Maybe she's in the parking lot behind the building. It's where I'm headed anyway, because that's where I park my car. So I go back out the front door, then past the empty shopfront, the bank, and the financial office, until I reach the alley.

I walk down past the dumpster to the parking lot. I put my

bags in my car, and then I turn to face the rear of the building.

And to my surprise, the back door to the muffin shop is closed. Usually by this point in the morning, the ovens have heated up the place so much that Wanda leaves the door open to let things cool off. And the rich, warm scent of raisin bread flows out and fills the parking lot here.

Not now, though. It's closed.

Hm.

So I count the doors from right to left, to make sure I'm looking at the right one. You'd think it would be easy: five shopfronts and five doors. Just start at one end and count. But Bank Row is an old building, just like my building is, and the back stairways twist and turn to where things never end up where you think they're going. It's always funny to me how hard it is to figure out which rear door goes with which shopfront. And even if you've seen the doors a hundred times like I have, you'll still stare at them, thinking, 'That can't be the bank's rear door, can it?' Or 'That can't be the tile shop's rear door, can it?' - even though it is.

So I triple-count. And yes, that's Wanda's door, and it's closed. And she's not out back here now, so I don't know where she is.

And at this point, I wouldn't have enough time to talk to her this morning even if I did find her.

So I get into my car, and I drive out through the streets of Teabridge, with its old-fashioned street lamps. Yes - we call them street *lamps* - not street *lights*. I mean, they're electric street lights, like any town has, but they're in the shape of old gaslights from the 1800's. Some people think they're a bit too precious, but I like them. Maybe that's just because I work in a modern seventeen-story office building made of glass and polished steel, and these lights just seem so much warmer.

Don't get me wrong - as Wanda said, my job at TechTile Incorporated is a fine one. And I do feel lucky to have it. And the seventeen-story glass-and-polished-steel building is a beautiful thing in its own way. But as I drive out of Teabridge

Village and merge into the ant-line of cars on the interstate, I feel lucky knowing that, nine hours from now, I'll return back home to a very different time and place.

So if you ask me, we should make all the lights on every street in the village look like street lamps, not just those on Cottage Street. Heck, we have gas lines in Teabridge, so we could make them actual gaslights. And how stunning would actual gaslight flames look on a foggy March morning, or a snowy December evening?

I feel a glow in my heart just thinking about it.

Paradigms

For now, I drive up six miles of busy highway to my exit. And right off the exit is the driveway up to the office park's huge ant-colony lot. I leave my car and enter the third building from the right, passing the philodendron near the big bank of shiny steel elevators. I get in one of these elevators and press the button for the fifth floor, home of TechTile Incorporated.

I have a long walk down the center aisle to my desk along the rear wall - passing cubicles on the way. This walk is actually good for me because it's the one time I get a sense of the whole office. And today, things are… interesting. The first thing I notice is that everyone keeps making trips to the coffee machine. Lots of furtive glances. Lots of groaning. Lots of giggling. I piece together clues from the random bits of conversation I hear, and it's very easy to conclude that people stayed late at Saucy June's last night. As in really late, especially for a Monday. Everyone but me and Jannelle seems to be pretty hungover.

Before I get to my desk, I stop into the breakroom and make herbal tea. Danny from Sales says, "That tea is so good for you. I should try that. But - wow - after last night, I need all the caffeine I can get."

"Go for it," I say. And I know that expression went out of fashion before I was even born. But that's only fitting, because I listen to music from before I was born, and I watch movies from before my grandmother was born. And did I mention the lights on my street are in a style that's centuries old?

I sit at my cubicle and set myself up for the day, which begins with me just making myself comfortable.

I put my mug into the knitted sleeve I made for it. It's a sweater, basically. I like sweaters, if you haven't noticed. I'm wearing one now, after all, so I put one on my mug, too.

I take my day-planner from my bag. I've decorated the cover with paisley-shapes that I drew with a marker, and I laminated a capsule movie review of the 1939 version of *Wuthering Heights* onto the back.

I open the planner and find today's page. The date is written in swirling black letters because last New Year's day, I spent the morning labeling each page with a calligraphy pen. And I kind of want to write my to-do list for today in calligraphy, too. But Jannelle stops by to deliver some notes for the morning meeting, and even though she's nice and could care less about what kind of handwriting I use, I change over to regular block letters, putting a little box next to each item so I can check it off when I'm done. She smiles and moves along.

I look over the meeting notes, to plan my list of what I have to do to get ready for it. One of the items is 'Field Report,' which is the vague title they use for updates from the people who work outside the office. Including Aaron.

So does that mean he'll be at this meeting?

I hope not.

But I also hope he is.

You know what I mean?

At ten-thirty, I go into the meeting expecting it to be low-key and subdued, just like things in general have been around here this morning.

The meeting is far from subdued, though. Instead, the room is filled with five minutes of the constant chatter of everyone talking about what a wonderful time they had last night. Being together in this room has revived them and put them right back into the social mood.

Finally Jannelle says, "Alright, to the business at hand."

As everyone settles in, she nods to Drew, head of the field workers.

"So," Drew begins, "the question of the day is... if we're going to expand the Northern European market, how can we do that, given how established the competition is in that area? And to answer that, I want to start with what the travel crew learned at the international conference in New York last week."

At that moment, on cue, Aaron and Ashley walk in. They don't slip in, trying to stay unnoticed, like I would do. They don't apologize profusely for being late, like I would do. They walk right to their chairs and then stand behind them, and Aaron nods to Ashley.

"Right," Ashley says. "Well, I've been on the phone to a rep from Iceland, of all places. And we learned some things, the most interesting of which is the simplest: we lose business when we communicate within a nine-to-five, Eastern Standard Time zone framework, especially given how Northern Europe is increasingly focused on Southeast Asia. And Australia and New Zealand, too, for that matter. So, pretty much as different as you can get. Obviously, one of our challenges is to get beyond the hours-of-the-day and days-of-the week paradigms."

Okay.

And what does all that mean, you may ask?

If you're lost, I totally get it, because I'm pretty lost myself. I mean, I do actually understand *some* of it - especially about the expansion of the Asian markets, which makes me proud that I'm possibly getting better at this job. But I don't understand enough of it. So I smile, which buys me time to figure out what the rest means, especially the 'hours-of-the-day paradigm' stuff.

But for some reason, when I think about the hours of *today*, I get stuck in a memory from early this morning when I heard that noise, looked out my window, and saw Wanda just standing in her doorway. It didn't make sense at the time, but I dismissed it, thinking she was just opening her shop. But now I remember that her front door was open already by that point. I know that because I had walked right through it earlier when I went to buy my muffin.

And if the noise wasn't caused by Wanda unlocking her door, then something else must have made the noise, and she was coming out to find out what it was.

So what was it? What made the noise?

And that's what I end up trying to figure out, instead of how to expand textile sales in the northern European to Southeast Asian corridor, while the meeting continues all around me.

Finally Jannelle says, "Alright, so clearly we need to stay exactly on pace with the market now more than ever, which means knowing what's coming next." Her voice is so commanding that I shudder a little as I notice that she's been nodding to me as she talks. And have you ever totally daydreamed at a meeting only to be woken up by everyone looking at you, waiting for an answer to a question you didn't even really hear?

Well, that's me. Right now.

Everyone's looking at me. And the only way to get them to stop looking at me is to respond to Jannelle.

So I do that. I respond to Janelle.

"You want an update on the newest innovations in fabrics?" I say, taking a guess that's only slightly short of wild.

Please be right. Please be right.

"You got it," Jannelle says.

Yes!

"I'll get right on it," I say, more than relieved.

Jannelle wraps up the meeting, and that's it. We're done in less than thirty minutes.

On the way out, Aaron smiles like he's proud of me for my small contribution there at the end, as opposed to the usual zero contributions.

And no, I do *not* know what to make of the fact that he's proud of me.

But I have my research task for the day, and it's always nice to have a clear purpose. So I go back to my desk to apply myself. High school teachers use that phrase, right? As in, 'To succeed in life, you have to apply yourself'?

Well, that's what I do. I apply myself to researching fabric made from sustainable innovation, which is one of the key 'areas of the future' in wearable textiles.

For example, they can now make jeans made from old jeans. And I don't mean they put a lot of patches in them. What I mean is that they grind up old jeans back into raw fiber - pulp, basically - and then make new thread out of it.

They do similar things with fabric made from the weirdest things, like pineapple, lotus, and - get this - coffee grounds. I have to keep from getting too excited about this fact because, would I buy a shirt made out of coffee-yarn? Yes, I would.

And if you could make me a sweater out of hot chocolate while you're at it, I don't think I'd ever take it off.

I work the full hour until noon, and then I stop and take my lunch outside. I sit on a bench on the strip of grass between the concrete parking lot and the steel-and-glass front-face of the building, and I watch people walk by - including some workers from TechTile.

"So nice that you sit out here," Rennie, the head of Media, says. And she means it, too, even though it's something she would never do. It's just like the way Danny said it's nice that I drink herbal tea, but still he reached for the coffee pot. I smile and nod.

The whole crew from Media is going to lunch together. I know some of them, so I could join them if I wanted. But I'm glad I packed my lunch. Saucy June's last night was enough socialization for me.

After they're gone, I actually have a surprisingly quiet moment. No cars move in the parking lot. A light breeze rolls over the grass. This bench is near a maple tree that gets good light and plenty of water from the in-ground sprinkler system, which keeps the trees rich and full of broad, deep green leaves. I love the shade I get from a lower branch that sticks out over the bench, while all around, the sun lights up the grass like an emerald carpet.

I finish my lunch, and I'm just about to close it up. But... what's this in the pouch? A chocolate-covered triple-chocolate oatmeal cookie?

Why, yes - it *is* a chocolate-covered triple-chocolate oatmeal cookie.

As I eat it, I think once more about Wanda, specifically her just standing there in the door to her shop. She was looking at something. Or looking *for* something.

The more I sit here, the more I'm convinced she must have been looking for the cause of that same noise I heard - the banging, or clanging, or whatever it was. A passing truck rumbling over cobblestone crosswalk? Someone slamming a door after delivering to the convenience store? Whatever it was, she heard it too, and she stepped onto the street to look around and figure out what it was.

Oh, well. I suppose it doesn't matter. I don't know why I keep thinking about it. It's just, when I sit in the front window in my apartment, I always do get the feeling that the Cottage Street end of Teabridge Village is my own little world, and I like to know what's going on in it.

And it's funny how some people can seem like they have only a small role in your life - just someone you see for two minutes in the morning - but really they have a very big role in your life. Wanda is a touchstone for me. I always feel better after I talk to her - always. I feel grounded. Some days, when everything is busy and rushing around, it seems like she's the only person I make eye contact with the whole day.

After lunch, I leave all these thoughts behind as I go deep into researching the agricultural base of South American countries. If banana fibers really do become a major source of fabric, we should probably know how the crops are doing this year.

I get so deep into research that I barely look up until the tinkling bell rings on my computer, telling me it's time for afternoon tea. I take a breath, rub my eyes, and then stand up to go to the breakroom. And this must be the first time I've looked up from my computer since I came back from lunch, because all of a sudden I realize how empty the office has become.

All morning people come and go, but after the daily meeting finishes in the late morning, people just leave. They go off to lunch and then to sales calls. Or off to meet people at Bradley airport down in Hartford. Or just off to work from home.

Moments like these are when I realize that we really are an international company, in our own small-city way. We have in fact gone beyond the hours-of-the day and days-of-the-week paradigm. There are no time zones here. For that matter, there is no 'here' here. We're everywhere.

The office holdouts - the only ones left who still physically exist in this space at this hour - are me, the receptionist, and the people in the accounting bloc. And Jannelle, of course.

I think that's why everyone around here likes parties so much. They spend so much of the work day away from the office or working from home, alone, that they start to miss each other.

At 4:55, I review my to-do list. I got pretty far today - more than two-thirds of the way through the 'innovations in fabrics' research. So I skip ahead to the last item on my list, which reads, 'Pack up and leave.'

Yes, the last item on my to-do list is to stop doing things.

So I do that. I stop.

I pack up my bag and I leave.

And I drive back up through the office park driveway to the access ramp for the Interstate, where I merge into the line of cars on the four lane road, and we flow together until I get off at the exit for the smaller state highway. A mile from Teabridge, this road narrows down to two lanes, and the buildings get smaller until they turn into houses.

I pull into downtown Teabridge - up into the alley across from my apartment, all the way through to the rear lot.

It's quiet back here. Wanda isn't here, and her rear door is closed. It's still hard to tell which door goes to which store. Bank Row was built as a factory, then a spa, and then finally broken up into the five storefronts that are here now. The end design is a mishmash of all its past configurations, and nothing is where you think it's going to be. The only reason I know for sure that Wanda's door is closed is that right now they're all closed. So I should just go up to my apartment. And I'm about to, but just out of impulse, I walk up close enough to the building so that I can look through the rear windows.

When I come to Wanda's, I can see all the way through into the front of the shop, though it's mostly just shadows from this angle. But are those trays just left out? It's so dark in there that it's hard to tell. I let my eyes adjust to the light, and I do think they're trays. That's not like Wanda to just leave things around like that.

Then I hear a vague, distant voice. Or I think I do, anyway. Is it from out on the street? A nearby neighborhood? Or is it... Wanda? It kind of sounds like Wanda.

No. It can't be. I'm probably just concentrating so hard on staring into her shop that my imagination is hearing any distant voice as though it's hers.

But... If that's the case, then I think my imagination is *feeling* things, too. Because something doesn't feel right. Am I alone back here? I must be alone. The Tile and Flooring shop is way over there, and that's usually pretty quiet anyway. The bank and the financial office are both closed, so they're all gone home. Wanda's is closed. The only other place in Bank Row is the empty storefront - which is, you know, empty.

So what's giving me this creepy feeling?

I don't know. And I'm not getting anywhere just standing here being creeped out, so I finally just drop it, and I go around through the alley and then across the street, up to my apartment.

I unload my things, and I make dinner: carrot-ginger soup, with a base of chicken stock and plain yogurt. It's smooth and rich - sharp from the ginger but a little sweet, too, from the carrots. It goes great with a couple of thick slices of the bread-machine bread I made on Sunday. Since I already ate the lopsided top slice, the rest is in that perfect round-cornered shape of the bread machine pan.

And I kind of miss the lopsided slice. I don't know why. It just seemed interesting. Different. So I cut my pieces for tonight crooked, on purpose.

I get ready to eat at the table - this small oak round top my aunt gave me. And I have a mismatched set of actual-silver silverware that I bought at a tag sale, with handles so swirly and ornate you'd think they were from Colonial times - or maybe some castle somewhere, especially since the swirls look like crowns. And I knitted my own placemat when I first took up the hobby last year, post-Aaron. In fact, I think it was my first finished knitted piece, because a simple rectangle is such an easy beginner project. Of course, even though it's easy, my version still has crooked stitches everywhere, but I think that just makes it kind of charming in its own way. I mean, I'm still not a great knitter, but if you want a sweater for your coffee mug or a wavy rectangle for a placemat, I'm your girl.

Despite all my warm thoughts about my small dinner table, I glance at the double-window, which faces north, and I can see to the left that the sun is angled to go down over the Edicom River. And that's a beautiful sight to see the orange sun in the western sky, along with flickers of its reflection off the river.

And wouldn't it be nice to sit in front of this window and eat my dinner as the sun goes down?

Yes, it would.

So I pull my lap desk from the side of my couch, and it's just the perfect size to fit my place setting. I add my soup bowl and a small plate with my thick-bread slices. And I grab SuperFuzz, just to make things extra comfy and cozy.

And... well... if you want to be extra-*extra* comfy and cozy, there's really no better way to do that than to get into your pajamas, is there? I usually wait until after dinner to get in my pajamas - which is still probably three or four hours earlier than most people change into their pajamas.

But it's what I want to do right now, so I do it. I get into my pajamas now, barely a half-hour after I got home from work. I settle into my easy chair, I put SuperFuzz back in my lap, and then I put the lap desk-turned-dinner-table on top. I eat and watch the sky go from yellow to orange to the blue-gray of evening. I stare at the moon in the northeast, looking so hazy-translucent I wonder if it's even there at all.

And speaking of things that aren't really there, I keep thinking about Wanda. If I'm honest, she's the real reason I'm sitting in front of this window now.

I was hoping to see her this afternoon so I could talk to her, at least to thank her for being so nice to me this morning. So now that I'm sitting in front of the window looking at the moon and the street lamps and just whoever is walking by, I also keep glancing at the muffin shop. There's no point to it, because Wanda is long gone for the day, but it's kind of like checking your phone for a message even though you know there's no realistic chance that it's come yet. You just *want* that thing, and it stays in your mind. And so you think, maybe if I just keep looking for it, it will suddenly appear.

Plus it really seems strange that Wanda wasn't there when I went down to see her the second time this morning.

Ooh - maybe she's a missing person. She could be, right?

I text Fi: *Is it true that a person has to be missing for 48 hours to be declared a missing person?*

She responds right away: *No.*

And now that the first contact is made, we go back and forth.

Me: *No? Really?*

Fi: *Yes, really.*

Me: *Oh.*

Fi: *You read a lot of mystery books.*
Me: *I know.*

I pause. She pauses too.

Then I press 'dial.' It rings twice, three times. Is she too busy to talk? I'd understand if she is, but I really hope she isn't.

After the fourth ring, she picks up.

I jump right in. "So how long *do* you have to wait?"

"How long do you have to wait to declare someone a missing person?" Fi says. "Is that what you're asking?"

"That's what I'm asking."

"If you have a real reason to be suspicious, don't wait at all," she says. "Especially with children."

"How about if it's an adult and you don't have a real reason - just a wild impulse?"

"Then sit on your hands until the wild impulse passes."

"Hey! That's what you tell Grace and Emmy when they're fidgeting too much. Someone's life could be at stake here."

"Hold on," Fi says. "Are we talking about a mystery book or an actual situation?"

"An actual situation," I say.

"And you have reason to believe someone's life is at stake."

"Well, no. Not actually."

"And what kind of tea did you have today?"

"In the morning, I had herbal tea."

"And this afternoon?"

"Um… Oolong."

"Oolong is black tea, isn't it? With caffeine."

"Alright, yes," I say. "You caught me. But just because my brain is a bit wired at the moment doesn't mean I'm completely crazy."

"No it doesn't," she says. Then I hear her kids in the background, and she adds, "But I have to go now, Sis."

"I know," I say. "Goodnight, Sis."

I click off, and I immediately text her a smiley face. Then a sleeping face with 'z's' coming out of its mouth.

Talking to Fi was a fun way to think about Wanda, and it distracted me from actually worrying about her. So I put my phone on night-time mode. I clean up my two dishes, I make some ginger-chamomile tea to counteract the Oolong, and then I climb right back into my easy chair.

I turn on the floor lamp, and I pick up *The Wayward Daughter*. And in the book, the girl keeps getting clues that her mother is still alive, but that she's just hiding. An old friend of her Mom's stops by one day, hands her a sweater in an old box, and says, 'Your Mom really wanted you to have this' - which is really weird because her Mom hated sweaters. It's crazy, I know - but apparently there are some people in the world who don't understand the natural beauty of sweaters. But it's clearly a clue to the mystery, and these clues add up to *something*, obviously. Unfortunately I'm too unfocused to put them together, and I keep dozing off - in and out. I always fall asleep at some point when I'm reading, but it happens especially early tonight. No surprise, given that I stayed at Saucy June's last night until - what time was it? Eight o'clock? No, I think it was even later. I think it was eight-ten.

Eight-ten!

Can you believe I stayed out that late?

And that wasn't even the end of the evening, because then Fi and I came back here to pajamas and SuperFuzz and sanity. And even though, yes, I'm kidding about eight o'clock being a late hour, it still took the wind out of me, because right in the middle of a chapter of *The Wayward Daughter*, I drop off to sleep here in the easy chair by the window, into a half-dream of old sweaters and missing persons. Fi and I are in a woodsy place, with water nearby, too. A pond or a lake or something. We're on an adventure, running through caves, trying to find someone. It's scary and thrilling at the same time, which makes a lot of sense, really, because it pretty much describes my childhood - especially after Mom left: me and Fi, together on some crazy caper.

In the dream, though, it's not just the two of us. There's one more - a third adventurer. I'd love to figure out who she is, because she feels so familiar and trustworthy. The trouble is, when I wake up at some point in the night, I can't remember her face or anything about her, except how comfortable it is to have her around.

I look out into the warm sepia half-light of the glowing streetlamps. Everything is still. And silent. And peaceful.

Except, wait a second, are those shadows moving down near the empty shop next to Wanda's?

I don't know, because the next thing I know I fall asleep completely, and the rest of my night is full of dreams about - and this is weird - some guys in the empty storefront next to Wanda's. In the dream, they're opening a shop there. And they're not nice people.

This dream kind of feels real, actually.

Like, really real.

Part Three: I Loved You Wednesday

"Hi there. I didn't mean to startle you," Wanda said. "It's just that it's been a few days now, and I thought I should say 'hi.'"

"Oh - thanks," he said. "And it's okay. You didn't startle me."

"That's good. My name's Wanda, by the way. And you are...?"

"I'm Nate."

"Hi Nate," she said. "What are you doing here?"

"Um... well... the guys..."

"The guys, what?"

"They said to wait, I think."

"You think," she said. "But you don't know?"

"No," he said. "I don't know. They don't tell me much, to be honest."

"Well, are you hungry? Do you want a muffin while you wait? I haven't made any new ones yet this morning, but I have a few left from yesterday."

"Oh..." he said. He clearly did want a muffin. But his eyes darted around nervously, and finally he just said, "I'd better not."

Interesting. He was a young adult - maybe nineteen years old - but his manner in this moment was more like that of a little kid.

A scared little kid.

"Nate," she said. "What I'm about to tell you is none of my business, but if you don't mind my saying..."

His eyes widened: he wanted to hear what she was going to say.

But she never got to say it, because at that moment, a door opened - the one to the stairs that led to the empty store next to her muffin shop.

Two men stepped out.

These were the 'guys' Nate was referring to.

And right away, she knew he was right to be scared.

Remote Possibilities

I wake up kind of suddenly. I say 'kind of,' because I think some noise wakes me up - even though I don't actually remember hearing any noise. Has that ever happened to you where you hear something while you're asleep and it's enough to wake you up, but by the time you finally do wake up, the noise stopped and you can't even tell if you heard it in the first place?

Anyway, what I do know for sure is that, all at once, I'm awake.

I'm sitting slumped down in my easy chair, with SuperFuzz all mounded up on top of me.

I take out my dream journal and try to sort out my dreams - writing down what I think they're about. I start with the dream about going on adventures with Fi.

What does it mean? Hm. The woods and the water remind me of how, when I was young, our family did go to a lake house every summer.

As for the caves in that dream, I'm not sure, because I don't remember there being any caves at the lake house, but Fi and I would roam around making up pretend adventures - some of which surely involved caves. Fi called us the two Musketeers, which I didn't understand at the time. But I liked the sound of it. I liked the sound of anything that joined me and Fi as partners.

And what's interesting is that, in the dream, I'm really into the adventure - which is how I used to be back then. In fact, in the dream I'm even kind of the leader, though I was never the leader in real life - not with Fi being five years older than I am.

But dreams are like that, aren't they? They're airy and you can't quite grab onto what they're about. And the more I try to grab onto this one and figure it out, the more analytical I get - which makes the dream fade away into one vague dream-wash. It's just like how my memory of seeing those shadows on Cottage Street in the middle of the night blends in with everything else, more and more, until I have no idea whether it actually happened or not.

So it must not have happened.

Of course not, right? Shadowy figures roaming the night? Not in Teabridge.

I lean back and look at the old analog clock above the stove. Almost eight o'clock. Ouch. If I'm going to be at work by nine, I need to get moving. No time to get a muffin and bring it back here to sit and read and wake up slowly, like I usually do. I'll have to grab one on my way to the car and eat it during the commute.

I blow through a shower and put on the quickest outfit I own: slacks and a pullover.

I grab my bags and walk down to the street. And as I get ready to cross, I look over at Bank Row, and I see newspaper pages taped over the windows of the empty shop front next to Wanda's.

What?

When did that happen?

Hm. I didn't know that place had been rented. So I go right up to the window, but every inch of it is covered with newspapers. Even the cracks between the pages are blocked with masking tape, so there's nothing to see.

I walk over to Wanda's front window. Nothing to see here, either: it's empty of people.

Yet there's a tray of muffins still on the counter. I can see them from here. Is that the same tray that was there last night? No, it couldn't be.

Hm, again.

I try the door; it's locked. Seems to be.

So I try harder. I shake it a little, and it opens. *Was* it locked, or just a little sticky?

I lean in and call out: "Wanda?"

I hear her voice. At least I think I do. But it's that distant thing again. It could be anyone's voice, from anywhere. So I put one foot through the door.

"Wanda?" I call, louder this time.

Now I hear nothing at all.

I walk all the way in, and it feels like I'm sneaking in. I mean, I actually creep - taking exaggerated, crouching steps, though I don't know why. Wanda wouldn't mind in the least if I came in and served myself. I've certainly done that before. And I *did* call out to her twice already. But it's so quiet in here.

She must be out back.

I walk to the rear door that leads to the back parking lot - the same door I looked through yesterday on my way home from work. It's locked, both the doorknob and the deadbolt. But why would Wanda keep both of these locked at this point in the morning when she's usually in and out so much?

I go to the entrance to the basement and call one more time: "Wanda?" But this time I say it at only half-volume, because something about the dark stairway makes me hesitate - like all the sudden it feels like I'm really starting to pry too deep into her business, invading her privacy. Because if she is down there, then she's busy working - rotating her stock, or who knows what. I'd probably just scare the daylights out of her if I pry any further.

So I just drop the whole idea of trying to find her. Instead, I grab a muffin from the counter, and I leave my money next to the register.

On my way out of Wanda's, I pause again in front of the empty storefront that's now, apparently, no longer empty. And it's still really strange that I didn't hear anything about this place being rented. I mean, I don't know how I *would* hear. I'm not on the zoning board and I'm not in the Chamber of Commerce. But it feels like I should have known. Like, Wanda would have mentioned it. Or Sheila from the convenience store, or Cynthia from Yarned. Cynthia would have known for sure, because she follows everyone's business.

And this all feels… not right.

I walk around back to the parking lot. A van sits near the rear doors. The words 'Carpentry and Repair' are painted on the side in plain, easy-to-read block letters, along with a phone number. Above that is a swirling logo and a name - Dennis Walt, or something like that. This part is written in airbrushed script, so it's hard to tell. It's like someone tried too hard to make the van look like the front of a heavy metal rock band t-shirt or something, but all they've really succeeded in doing is to make it nearly illegible. If I stared at it long enough, I could figure out what it actually says, but now I notice there's a man sitting in the driver's seat. And he's looking at me. He's not glaring, but just looking - like he knows me or something. So I can't help but kind of look back at him. Does he seem familiar to me? I can't tell. And now he's checking his phone for a message or something. Or did he just stop looking at me *when* I looked at him?

Anyway - enough of this. So there's a carpenter's van in my parking lot. Who cares? I have to get to work.

But on the drive in to work, I *do* care.

Because I keep thinking about the store - the no-longer-empty store next to Wanda's. Normally, it's fun when a new shop arrives in town, with everyone peeking through the window each time they pass, watching as the 'for rent' sale comes down and the place evolves. As it gets painted, and furniture or shelves or counters are installed, we all ask each other, *Is it going to be a restaurant? A dentist? A hardware store?* It's like a kids' game where the picture starts out blurry, and as it slowly gets clearer, you try to be the first one to guess what it is.

In a way, I'm hoping it's going to be a cafe because I love them. But I wouldn't want anyone giving Wanda competition. So a retail shop would be my next preference. I could go onto the internet to see if there have been any announcements in the business page of the Leighton Register website.

But it's funny - when it comes to stores opening on Cottage

Street, the person I'd really want to talk to about all of this is Wanda. And she's missing.

Wait - no. She's not *missing*. Is she?

No. Not missing. She's just not… there.

At work, I get immersed right back into the 'next wave of textile innovations' project - completing the research phase and preparing to work up the full report. It takes me the whole morning, so I don't get a chance to look up whether the storefront across the street was rented or sold or anything.

At lunch, I go outside to sit on the bench. And I lean back and watch people come and go - calm and normal. The one bit of excitement comes when I get caught in one of these flash rains we get around here sometimes. It's an Edicom Valley thing. The clouds get stuck between the mountains and do strange things. That's my theory, anyway. And what happens is, it could be sunny one moment, then rain, and then sunny again - all within fifteen minutes.

I want to stay here on the bench and sit out the shower. The tree is blocking at least some of the rain, and the temperature is still pleasantly mild, so it would be kind of fun to get wet. But TechTile is just not the kind of office where you can return from lunch half-soaked, dry your hair with paper towels in the bathroom, and then go back and sit at your desk - at least not without half the office coming over to you and saying, "What happened to *you*?"

So I duck under the cover of the front foyer of our building, and I eat the rest of my lunch standing up, just to breathe the outside air for a little longer. And when I'm done eating, I go to close up my lunch bag, and I notice the inside pouch where I sometimes hide little presents to myself, like the triple-chocolate oatmeal cookie from yesterday. But the pouch is empty today, of course. There's no surprise baked good from Wanda's shop, because Wanda wasn't at the store when I went in this morning.

And I know I've said this about twenty five times this

morning, but I'm going to say it again: that's weird, alright? It's weird that all this happened on the very same morning that the store next door had newspaper up on the windows. I mean, that just has to mean something, doesn't it?

I go back to my desk with a few minutes left of my lunch break, and now I do go online. I start by checking whether Wanda's shop has a landline, because if it does, I could just look up the number and call her to see if maybe she was just late for work this morning and has now finally arrived. But I don't find any landline number - which makes sense, because all I've ever seen her use is her cell phone. So next I check real estate sales in Teabridge Village for a listing on the empty storefront next to Wanda's. I see a few houses for sale, but no stores - which makes sense because it's probably not a sale. I know the guy who owns Bank Row because he also owns my building, and I don't think he'd sell a unit outright, since everything else he owns is a rental.

So that's another dead end. And now it's one o'clock anyway. Back to work.

And I do get right back into my 'future of textiles' project, flowing through it to the point where, by four o'clock, I'm well ahead of schedule.

On Wednesdays, we close an hour early, as a little treat for the employees since this is, supposedly, the hardest day of the week - which is a funny tradition to hold on to given that, as usual, people began dispersing after lunch to go to meetings or work by remote, so what's the difference between four o'clock or five o'clock when almost everyone's gone by two-thirty?

Today is one Wednesday when I'd actually like to stay until five, to resume the internet searching I started at lunch. But before I can really get into it, Jannelle and the accounting twins - the only ones left in the office besides the evening cleaning crew - come over to my desk at three fifty-nine and just stare at me. There's no actual rule that says I couldn't stay later than they're staying, but there's an unwritten one that the four of us have: if one of us stays, we all have to stay. And the converse is that if three of us are all packed and ready to leave, then the fourth one - in this case, me - should leave, too.

And three people staring at me is exactly three more people than I can handle staring at me. Plus, Wanda should still be in her shop at this hour, finishing up a few last-minute things after closing time. In this day and age, despite all our technology, sometimes the best way to find out if someone is okay is still to just go ask them.

So I leave with the group, and I head back to Teabridge.

Windows

I drive home through afternoon traffic, weaving in and out of lanes and waiting an extra light cycle at each intersection until I get to the quieter streets of Teabridge, where there are hardly any stop lights at all.

And when I come around the curve to my stretch of Cottage Street, I see a dark van parked outside the empty storefront, with a man on a ladder outside of it.

I really should stop calling it the empty storefront, because something's going on there now, for sure. It's hard to tell while I'm driving, but it looks like the newspapers are gone from the front window, and it's well on the way to becoming an actual store.

I drive through the alley to the parking lot, and to my surprise, there's another van back here - a beat up old white one. But I can't tell what it's doing here or even which store it's attached to because there's that whole thing about how Bank Row was first a factory, then a spa, and then finally this row of five storefronts. The end design is a mishmash of all its past configurations, and nothing is where you think it's going to be.

But the front of the building is easy enough to understand, so I carry my too-many work bags through the alley back to the street. The man on the ladder is using a pneumatic nailer connected to a hose that snakes across the sidewalk - all the way up into a compressor in the back of the dark van. And I now recognize the van as the same one I saw this morning belonging to Darren Walt, or whatever the guy's name is. The compressor kicks on just as I approach, and then the generator kicks on, too. And on top of all that racket made by the two motors, the nail gun makes a startling pop like a pistol shot each time the man puts in a new nail.

So to avoid all this commotion, I walk out into the street,

which gives me a good view of the sign that's now above the door, though calling it a 'sign' is being too generous: it's just the words 'Dollar Discount' hastily painted on a piece of scrap wood.

And the whole time I'm staring at the sign, the man on the ladder is staring at me.

I nod a 'hello,' and I keep walking past him to Wanda's shop. And I see, taped right here to the inside of her door, a note.

It reads...

> On Vacation.
> Back next week.
> - *W. Beecher*

What?

Beecher?

I mean, that might be Wanda's last name, because it does sound kind of familiar. But she calls everyone she knows by their first name, and if you ask her what her name is, she says, "Wanda." That's it. Not "W. Beecher."

Plus, but if she was going on vacation, she would have told me. I know I'm just a customer - not a family member or anything. But she would have told me.

So I try the door. It's locked - really locked this time. Jostling doesn't do a thing.

I stick my face right up to the glass and cup my hands around my temples to block off the glare. And all I see inside is shadows. So again I wait for my eyes to adjust, and I think I see the very same muffin tray on the counter - the one that's just been sitting there for two days now. I'm concentrating so hard that I barely notice when the carpenter's generator turns off. But I definitely notice when the compressor kicks off, too, because all the sudden I can hear again. And breathe, for that matter.

And maybe I can even think again, too - like about what's going on with Wanda.

Because I'm really starting to think that something *is* going on with her.

But my thinking is interrupted by a voice. "Hi Lizzie."

It's the man on the ladder.

How does he know my name?

I look up at him, and he looks down at me, which apparently he's been doing the whole time.

And that should freak me out, but his expression is relaxed and easy, like he knows who I am and is glad to see me - which is nice. But it would be a whole lot nicer if I knew who *he* was.

I mean, he does look kind of familiar. But I don't know any Darrens, do I?

I look at the big logo on the van. And from this close proximity, in the full afternoon light, it's easier to decipher that it doesn't say 'Darren Walt.'

It says 'Devin Wahl.'

And yes, I do know him. Or I knew him, anyway. We went to school together over in Leighton, where I grew up. He's a year older than I am. I remember that because we took physics together when I was in the eleventh grade, and we both sat in the back. I think he felt out of place in a class with younger kids. You know how it is when you're in high school: any little difference like being a year behind in a single class can make you stand out, even though it's really nothing in the grand scheme of things. Remembering all that now makes me feel bad for him. I think he even tried to become friends with me, but I was too shy to even notice at the time.

And all this explains the look he gave me this morning, because he obviously recognized me right away.

And now that I've finally recognized him back, he can actually talk to me.

"Been a while, huh?" he says.

I nod, because it *has* been a while. Eleven years or more, almost half our lives. He's got his own business, apparently, so it looks like he's recovered from his physics class setback. I give him credit for that, even if his van's huge, air-brushed logo does look a little teen-boyish.

"Hi Devin," I say.

He smiles when I use his name, as though I've actually remembered it on my own instead of reading it from the van.

The smile is sweet and warm, and it encourages me to take a chance.

"The owner of this shop is named Wanda," I say. "She's a black woman, late forties. Have you seen her?"

"Not at all," Devin says. "The note says she's on vacation."

"Yeah, I see the note. But it wasn't here this morning. You've been working here all day, haven't you?"

He nods and rolls his eyes.

"What's that look for?" I say.

"I've been here all day, but I can't call it 'working,'" he says. "It's kind of a weird job."

"Why? What did they hire you to do?"

"They told me to change the casing here on the front of the store," he says, "but look..."

He shows me the existing window trim - a classic white grooved strip. Then he shows me the new trim he's putting up to replace it. It's the same. *Maybe* there's an extra groove in the replacement trim, or maybe there's one less groove. I can't really tell from here. But either way, the point is that nobody could without looking closely. And if nobody can tell the difference, what's the point of changing it?

"Why are you doing that?" I say, point blank.

He shrugs.

"Didn't you ask them?" I say. "You should ask them."

Interesting. I don't usually tell people what to do. But I'm telling him what to do.

And now I remember that we didn't just sit near each other during that class we took together; I tutored him, too. Physics was easy for me (I have no idea why) but he never could quite get it. And I used to get frustrated with him. I mean, not *angry*-frustrated. But I think I used to enjoy pushing him around a little, which is *so* not 'me.'

And, not that this makes it right, but he doesn't seem to mind my bossy-ness now, either, because he does answer me. "I asked them about their plans for renovation," he tells me, "I could probably give them some good ideas for it. But they don't seem to want me to know any of their plans at all. They just keep giving me meaningless tasks, all of which involve the air compressor, for some reason. Gets pretty hard on the ears, even with headphones."

"Dollar Discount, huh? What does that mean?"

"They sell stuff."

"Okay. *What do they sell?*"

"Toys, I think. And clothes, definitely clothes."

"Is the place open yet?"

"Not officially."

I reach for the door handle.

"Wait, what are you doing?" he says.

"I'm going in."

"Yeah?" he says. "You sure?"

"Why wouldn't I be sure?" I say.

He opens his mouth, but he can't quite think of an answer.

So I go in.

The once-empty store has two folding tables set up as islands in the middle, with shelves lining the three inside walls.

But it's an exaggeration to say that they're 'lining the walls' because there's only one shelf on each one. And they're not big permanent shelves, either; they're those three-foot-wide plastic towers you get at the home store, making the place look more like a tag sale than an 'establishment.'

So what's on these shelves and tables? Well, Devin was right. It's… stuff. Boxes of stuff. And by 'boxes,' I mean *boxes*: brown cardboard shipping containers with the tops cut off. Pretty jaggedly cut off, too.

I look inside one of them. It's a pile of packages of what looks like Silly Putty in those purple plastic eggs, with a blue cardboard backing encased in clear plastic. Except the label on the backing doesn't say 'Silly Putty.' It says 'Slimy Puddy,' in swirly, close letters, so you don't notice right away that it's a knock-off product. And the kids in the drawing look more freaked out than they do happy. Their eyes are big and startled-looking, and their mouths are twisted into maniacal smiles.

Another box has t-shirts in it, and the top shirt has a logo: "I'm all that!" written in splashy letters. I pick up the shirt. It's made of some kind of polyester - I *think*. I mean, I work in textiles, and still it's got me puzzled. It's not a fabric you'd want next to your skin, that's for sure, because it's not just rough, it's actually abrasive. You could scrub a dirty saucepan with it, maybe, but don't wear it, whatever you do.

And I guess I'm paying a little too much attention to the shirt - holding it up to my eye, examining the weave, rubbing it with my thumb and pointer finger - because it takes me a moment to notice that someone else has come into the room. A young man with dark hair and serious dark eyes.

And those eyes are looking right at me.

"What do you want?" he says.

"Just browsing…"

"Who told you to come in here?"

"No one. I just came in," I say. And all at once, I don't want to be here anymore.

"Um… It sounds like you're not open yet," I add, backing up slowly. "So maybe I'll just…"

Then I hear a voice - someone coming up the stairs. "Hey Cory, do you know what we're supposed to do with…" It's a second guy - younger, with pale skin. Cory glares at him, angry at having his name used in front of a stranger.

But the young guy doesn't notice that. Instead, he notices me standing here, and he stops short, surprised. Alarmed, even. Then he leans his head back toward the stairs. "Griff?" he calls out. "Griff, you might want to come up here."

Out of the blue, Cory punches the young guy in the shoulder. It startles this younger one so much that he doesn't even get angry; he's just shocked. I have the same reaction.

"What was that for?" the young guy says, when he recovers. "I didn't say his whole name. I just said..."

Then a third guy emerges from the entrance to the stairs. "Nate - what the..."

So now I know all their names. And I wish I could learn even more about them - like who they are and what they're up to - but I feel like I need to get out of here, right now.

How do I do that? I can't just run, because that would just be too weird, even for me. I've retreated from socially awkward situations plenty of times (several times a day, on average), but I usually wait until no one's looking at me, and then I slip out the side door. There's pretty much always a side door in any situation by the way, if you know where to look. Trust me: as the queen of wallflowers, I know about side doors.

Unfortunately, the 'disappear into the wallpaper' option is not available to me at the moment, because all three of these guys are staring at me. Griff even leans toward me with a nasty expression, breathing heavily through his nose.

And inside, I'm thinking, 'Oh, no - oh, no - oh, no...' I mean, I don't show this on the outside, of course. One of the first things they teach you in women's self-defense is to keep calm. Keep your head. So I do that. I keep my head.

But they also say that your best chance of staying safe in a violent situation is not to get into it in the first place. So maybe I *should* just run, no matter how suspicious it looks.

The problem is that Griff's looking like he's not going to let me out of here that easy, and he glances at his two helpers to back him up.

They start to move toward me, and I'm thinking, *Is this it? Are they going to attack me?* Then a loud banging sound shatters the tension.

It's Devin at the front window, nailing the trim with a heavy ball-peen hammer.

The interruption snaps Griff out of whatever bad thing he

was about to do to me - *if* he was about to do something bad to me. I mean, I still don't have proof that these guys are up to anything at all, besides opening a store that sells really cheaply-made things.

But I do know how I feel. Which is bad.

And the feeling gets even worse, because now that Griff knows Devin is watching, he puts on a smile that's even creepier than the intimidating glare from a moment ago.

"Cory here will help you," he says - meaning, *I guess*, that I should buy something?

I look around, but I don't want one of the t-shirts. And I certainly don't want any Slimy Puddy.

A bit of red flannel sticks out of a box on one of the central tables, so I grab it, because if it's flannel, it can't be too bad, whatever it is. And I certainly wouldn't mind if it was, you know, *pajamas*.

It's not pajamas, but it *is* a flannel shirt - which is the next best thing. And it's in my size, too, which is to say that it's way too big for me. It's going to be super baggy, and the sleeves will cover my hands just like I want them to do.

"How much?" I say.

"Ten dollars," Cory says.

I'm definitely paying with cash, because there's no way I'm giving these guys my credit card number. So I reach in my pocket and pull out the only bill I have on me.

"Oh," I say, when I see that it's a five.

"Did I say ten?" Cory says. "I meant five."

I grimace, because that's very weird. Five dollars is way too little for any legitimate business to charge for a shirt.

So… is this stolen goods or something? Is the whole place a money-laundering operation?

"It's a grand opening sale," Griff says, when he sees my hesitation. "We haven't even got the register working. Call it a 'first customer discount.'" And okay, that *could* be a good explanation, except that I don't see any register anywhere, never mind a not-yet-working one.

I hand Cory the bill, and he snatches it out of my hand, so now I'm *really* ready to get out of here. I don't wait for them to put the shirt in a bag - not that anyone was reaching for one.

But as soon as I put my hand on the doorknob, Griff calls out to me.

"Miss," he says, in a hard tone. "You shouldn't come into places that aren't open yet."

I freeze. Everything freezes. It's like the air itself freezes.

I'm guessing that telling him the front door was in fact unlocked would be beside the point, so the only thing to do is to just leave.

When I finally get outside, I slip around into the foyer of Wanda's shop, and after fifteen or twenty breaths, I calm down enough to notice that Devin is still right outside the discount store, up on the ladder with the nail gun in his hand. He looks at me, relieved - as though, now that I'm safely out of the store, he can finally breathe again, too.

"What's going on with those guys?" I ask him.

He pulls a white mask from his tool belt and slips it on, just so the guys inside the store won't know that he's talking to me. And I hate to criticize his espionage skills, but he needs to learn to stop looking right at the person he's pretending not to talk to.

"I don't know what's going on with them, but you need to be more careful," he says.

"Fine with me," I say. "I'm going back to my apartment."

"Hey," Devin says, still behind me on the ladder. "Hey!"

I stop and turn back. "What?"

"If you're going to your apartment," he says, "don't walk straight across to it, okay?"

"Why? Do you know something, or don't you?"

"I don't know anything for sure," he says. "I'd just rather they didn't know where you live."

"Wait - how do *you* know where I live?"

He looks away. Is he blushing?

"Have you been watching me?" I say.

"No!" he says. "I just noticed, okay? I work alone out here. I have a lot of time to notice things."

"All right, all right," I say. "I'm not saying you're stalking me or anything. I'm just asking."

"Good, because I just want to see that you get home safely."

"Well… thank you," I say. And as I begin to walk more casually up the street, not directly across to my building, I glance back and I see that he's hopped down off the ladder and moved in front of the discount shop's front door, presumably to block the men if by any chance they were going to come after me - which is really unnecessary, given how open and public the street is.

But it's still kind of, you know, *nice*.

I walk down the block, glancing back every once in a while at Devin, who keeps giving me these 'sideways looks' that are actually super-conspicuous frontways-glares. And boy, he *really* needs to improve his undercover skills if we're going into the detective business together.

I mean, not that we *are* going into the detective business. I'm just saying.

And actually, for that matter, if the discount store guys are up to something, how do I know Devin isn't in on it with them?

I don't know that. He was a nice enough guy in high school, but that was a decade ago. Who knows what he's become in the meantime?

So, just to be extra safe, I walk all the way around the block to throw them all off, and then I head back up the street from the opposite direction. When I get close to my apartment, I duck behind a parking meter to lay low - one of those short, thin poles with the hand-crank meter on top. And *why* do I bother to 'duck behind' something that still leaves ninety percent of me exposed? I don't know why, but I do.

Miraculously, it works, because the discount store guys are still in the store, as far as I can tell, and Devin is kind of looking around for me, so he seems none the wiser. And now I see his unguarded expression - his 'real' expression - which isn't harsh or, quite frankly, mean like the discount store guys.

He looks concerned for me.

He takes a few more breaths, waiting to see if everything has finally settled down. And then he returns to his nailing.

With the nail gun.

Not the hammer.

And that's interesting, because just a few minutes ago in the discount store, I had that strange, tense moment when it felt like Griff and his boys were about to do something bad to me, and they only stopped when they heard Devin's hammering.

Except Devin hasn't been using a hammer for this project; he's been using a nail gun, which tells me that he used the hammer just to make that racket on purpose to interrupt whatever Griff was thinking of doing to me.

And that makes me just a little more sure that, yes, I can trust this guy - even if his undercover-operative skills do need serious improving.

Dimming of the Day

Up in my apartment, I hang up my jacket and put my work bags by my desk. Then I change out of my work clothes. I pretty much have to, because my breath is still short and my heart is pounding. I really need to get comfortable.

I reach for a pair of jeans and a sweatshirt. And then I think, well, if I'm going to get comfortable, maybe I should get *really* comfortable and just put on… you know… my pajamas.

I choose my blue-striped ones because they're freshly washed and, more importantly, freshly dried and at their height of thickness and fuzziness.

When I get them on, I hug myself, just to feel their warmth. And I finally exhale for real.

I push the easy chair even closer to the window, and I sink down into it, pulling SuperFuzz over me, making a hooded shawl, basically. I peek through the hole in the hood, and I see that Devin is packing up and leaving for the day. It's after 5:00 now, so that makes sense.

I can't tell if anything is happening inside Wanda's shop, because the dimming afternoon light hits her front window in a weird way, and all I see is the reflection of the cars that pass by on the street every once in a while.

As for the discount store, something's definitely going on inside there. Now that Devin is gone, I can see shadows moving, and I can even hear voices through my partially open window. They're vague, but I can hear them. It's those three men arguing, probably. Or most likely Griff shouting orders at the other two. I'm getting a strong sense that Dollar Discount is not what you'd call a healthy work environment. If nothing else, this whole thing is making me appreciate life at TechTile Incorporated.

And now, what's this? That rusty old white van with tinted-windows that I saw in the back parking lot rolls up to the front of the discount store. Then it stops and idles, loudly.

Within thirty seconds, Griff comes out. And now he's

definitely angry. He puts his hands up in a 'What the heck are you doing?' gesture. And he obviously wants to yell that, too, but he restrains himself out here in the exposure of Cottage Street.

He approaches the front passenger-side window to scold the driver some more, but before he gets there, something stops him.

A voice.

It's Cynthia from the Yarned knitting shop, calling to him from across the street.

He wants to ignore her, but Cynthia is not one to be put off easily.

She brushes off all his non-verbal cues, crossing the street and heading right for Griff. And before she gets even halfway across, she starts chatting to him. He smiles and nods, though it's obviously painful for him to be stuck in a conversation with Cynthia when he'd much rather be yelling at the van driver.

I open my window a little more, carefully and quietly. Then I kneel down on the floor right next to the window, and I put my ear up next to the three-inch opening. I can't quite hear the words they're saying over the racket of the van's engine, but as far as I can tell, it's mostly pleasantries.

But what's helpful is that Cynthia, in her distant New England politeness, never gets any closer than ten feet from him, which works for me because they have to raise their voices - enough that, despite the background noise, I can still pick up most of the words.

"So glad to see someone making improvements," Cynthia says. "Other shop owners around here are just a little too content to leave things the way they are."

She's referring to Wanda and her muffin shop, of course. She's always had a weird rivalry with Wanda that I've never completely figured out. And to be clear, when Wanda first opened the muffin shop, Cynthia did just the opposite of what she's doing now: she complained about the changes Wanda made, saying she liked things just the way they were.

Griff responds with a simple, "Yup" - clipped short, which is what he'd like to do to the whole conversation.

"And… Dollar Discount?" Cynthia says, not in the least bit discouraged. "What is it you'll be selling?"

"A little bit of everything," he says.

"Right. Of course," she says. "I'm sure you'll figure it out as you go along."

What? Cynthia wouldn't normally let anyone get away with an answer as vague as 'a little bit of everything.' But I guess if encouraging him is a way to make a dig at Wanda, then it's worth it to her.

"Yeah," he says. "Lots to do."

"Oh, okay. I'll leave you to it," she says. "So nice to meet you."

I could say she's finally gotten the hint that Griff wants to be left alone, but I know Cynthia. She's had the hint the whole time; she's just chosen to ignore it. I watch her retreat back into her shop, and Griff watches her too, sizing her up and considering whether she's trouble or not. I guess he decides she isn't trouble, because eventually he rolls his eyes. Then he approaches the side window of the van and leans into it, to resume his favorite hobby of yelling.

I definitely can't hear this new conversation, but I can *almost* see the driver through the tinted side window. I think it's Nate - the young, naive guy. I try to look closer, but from way up here, I can't look closer. I can just look harder.

Should I go down? No, I can't. I'd have to get dressed into actual clothes, for one thing. Re-dressed, that is. And if I did go down there, I don't know how I'd keep them from seeing me coming out of the door right across from them. And I definitely don't want that to happen now - not after they basically caught me snooping around their shop.

So I go to my closet and fetch out my bird watching binoculars so that I can…

Spy on them?

No. That's not what I'm doing. Spying sounds wrong.

All I want to do is just look at them from a distance without them knowing. Which, okay, is pretty much the definition of spying.

So… wait - am I really going to do this?

Yes. For Wanda, I'm really going to do this. I just hope I'm right in my suspicions.

By the time I get back to the window, Griff has stopped talking to the driver, who I can now see with the binoculars is definitely Nate. Griff goes to the back of the van, takes out some flattened cardboard boxes, and slams the door. He scowls and yells at Nate one more time. Then Nate pulls down the street and out of sight, as Griff brings the unassembled boxes into the store.

And that's it. It's quiet for a while.

A long while.

Okay.

For dinner, I have leftover soup and leftover bread, which I bring back to my stakeout point, formerly known as the easy chair. I balance both the bowl and plate on the lap desk, but it's hard to manage all that and still hold my binoculars at the same time. So I move the coffee table right next to the chair, turning it into just a huge end table. And on it I have a water bottle, my bird watching binoculars, a stack of books, and a notebook.

While I eat, I keep a watchful eye on the street below.

And since everything remains quiet, I text Fi:

> Me: *What are you doing?*
> Fi: *The dishes.*
> Me: *Can you talk? Kids around?*
> Fi: *Joe's doing bath-time.*

I call.

"Something is going on here," I tell her. "Wanda from the

muffin shop hasn't been around for two days now."

"So she's your forty-eight hour missing person?"

"Maybe," I say.

"I'll take that as a 'yes,'" she says. "So if she hasn't been around, who's been working at the shop?"

"No one. That's my point."

"Really? My gosh, how did you manage without your daily muffin this morning?"

I know she's teasing me, but I don't care.

"Well, I did have a muffin this morning," I say, "because the shop was open. Or at least I was able to get into it and get a muffin."

"What do you mean, 'at least I was able to get into it'?" she says.

"Nothing," I say. "I just, you know, jiggled the door a lot, and I eventually got in."

"*Lizzie!*"

"I just wanted a muffin," I say.

"Really. And you got one."

"Yes. But it was a day-old muffin."

"Oh, I see. A *day-old* muffin," she teases me. "Right. Now I understand why you're upset."

"This isn't about the muffin. It's about Wanda. She wasn't there. And the shop is definitely locked now, with no sign of her anywhere."

"When was the last time you actually saw her?"

"Yesterday morning."

"So not even two full days," she says. "Maybe she's just home sick with a cold."

"She's never sick."

"No one's *never* sick."

"Okay, but there's this weird note on the door of her shop. It says she's gone on vacation. I wrote it down, word-for-word. It says, 'On Vacation. Back next week.' And it's signed, 'W. Beecher.'"

"So there it is," Fi says. "Mystery solved. She's on

vacation."

"No. No way. She would have told me if she was going on vacation."

"Why would she tell you?"

"We're friends."

"Friends?" she says. "Actual friends?"

"Um… kind of."

"Have you hung out in any capacity besides brief chats at the shop?"

"No."

"Do you know where she lives?"

"No."

"Do you know her last name?"

"Yeah - it's Beecher."

"Right. Of course, you just said that," Fi says. "But did you know it before you saw this 'strange note'?"

"Um… no, not exactly," I say. "But… when I go into the shop each morning, she's really nice to me. And yesterday she called me her 'early morning friend.' Those were her words, not mine. So I just think that she would have told me."

"And you've had no sign at all from her since then, aside from the note?"

"No. And if she doesn't show up tomorrow, I don't know what I'll do."

"Okay, well, where are you right now? Are you at the window?"

"Yeah. I'm kind of camped out here, to tell you the truth."

"Is something happening now?"

"Not really. I think there's a light on at Wanda's. But I can't be sure. It's not dark enough to be sure yet."

"So go down and check."

"I can't. I'm in my pajamas."

"Already? Lizzie, my *kids* aren't even in their pajamas yet, and they're five and seven years old."

She doesn't know the half of it: I've been in my pajamas for two hours already.

"Well, maybe you should just go down and check all this out anyway, pajamas or no pajamas," Fi says. "Don't you always going to Wanda's before you even dress for the day?"

"Yes, except that's at five in the morning. No one's around at that hour to see me. But really, I think this is serious, and I think it needs something more than just me going down there, no matter how I'm dressed. Could you send someone?"

"Send who?"

"You know. A police officer."

"You want to call the police because your muffin was stale?" Fi says.

"I'm telling you, something's going on."

"What would the charge be, if we did send an officer?"

"Well, for one thing, there's this new store opening right next to Wanda's - a discount store. Three creepy, mean-looking men selling this crappy knock-off stuff. These guys are definitely up to something. You can bet on that."

"Have they done something illegal?"

"I don't know. That's what I'm trying to figure out. Can someone just go there and check out the situation? Who's that officer you're friends with? She met us at June's once."

"Well, I'm friends with a lot of officers. I work at the courthouse, remember. But I think you mean Julia Ramos."

"Yeah, her."

"Okay. And if I send Julia over, what will she find?"

"I don't know. Bad guys. Probably."

Fi laughs. "Well, maybe. But you need to think through this more rigorously if you want to be a detective."

"Who said I want to be a detective?"

"Hey, you called me. I didn't call you," Fi says. "Put yourself in her shoes. If Julia went over there right now, what would she actually, physically witness? I'm talking objective, observable facts. What would she see, hear, and even smell?"

"Well, she won't smell any baked goods, that's for sure. But she'll see Wanda's shop."

"You mean, she'll see the *front* of Wanda's shop. She can't go inside, right? Because it's locked?"

"Yes," I say. "I mean, it was locked as of this afternoon at four-thirty, anyway."

"So how's Julia going to get in?"

"I don't know. Break the door down."

"And, just to play along here, how is she justified in breaking the door down? She would need serious, hard evidence."

"Wanda's disappeared! How much hard evidence do you need?"

"We don't know that she's disappeared. All we know is that she wasn't at her shop at four-thirty. To break into a private business, you need what we call 'cause.' And once you have your cause, you bring it to a judge and try to get a warrant."

"But that takes days, doesn't it?"

"Sometimes - unless you have reason to believe that the situation requires immediate action."

"Like...?"

"A body lying on the floor in clear view through the window would be nice," she says. "Well, it wouldn't be *nice* to have a body on the floor, of course, but it would definitely be 'cause.' The more drastic and urgent, the better. So is there a body lying on the floor in clear view through the window?"

"Um. No. But I told you, I think that there's a light on in her shop."

"So what if there is?"

"Why would she have a light on if she's closed?"

"I don't know. Left it on by accident? Or left it on intentionally, for security? Plus, this is pointless because you don't even know if there *is* a light on."

"Hold on," I say. "It's going to get dark soon."

"That shadow thing?" Fi says.

"Yeah."

The 'shadow thing' is this interesting thing that happens each evening around here: the sun goes down over the hills in the southwest and casts a shadow over the town, and the light all around gets three shades dimmer in a matter of just minutes. Some days you swear you can see the actual movement of the shadow across Cottage Street. I watch it move now, and in one more minute, it will be dark enough to know whether there's a light on at Wanda's.

And so I wait.

And…

It turns out there is no light on at Wanda's.

"You're not talking," Fi says. "Does that mean you're seeing something?"

"No," I say. "The window is dark, just like it usually would be at this hour."

"You sound disappointed," Fi says.

"It's just… I really thought there'd be a light on, or some other clue."

"But you do understand that the goal here is for there to be nothing wrong?"

"Yeah, you're right. I guess."

"You guess."

"Listen, I know that something is wrong here," I say. "The lack of proof just makes it more frustrating. You're a forensic psychologist; you know about feelings."

"If by 'feelings' you mean emotions, you're right. But what you're talking about is a hunch."

"Police have those, too."

"If they're smart, they have theories," she says. "And they don't act on them; they test them."

"They test them."

"Yes. And you know what this all reminds me of, don't you?"

I do know. I don't even have to pause to think about it. "You're talking about the time at the lake house when we were little kids, right?"

"That's the one," Fi said. "Go ahead. Tell the story."

"What I remember is, we had a theory that the guy in the

next cabin was the Crazy Lake Killer," I say. "So we 'tested it' by telling him we thought we saw a fox near his chicken coop, just to have an excuse to peek through his windows while he went to check on it."

"Right. And what did we see when he was gone and we peeked through those windows?"

"Um…"

The image has stayed with me all these years: A single plate on the table with his half-eaten breakfast of beans and a crust of bread. An old flannel shirt with holes in the sleeve, draped over the back of the chair. A photograph on the wall of him and his deceased wife from their wedding day, decades ago.

My stomach drops every time I think of that photo.

"I'm still here, waiting for an answer," Fi says.

"Okay, fine," I say. "We found evidence of a harmless man who just wanted to live his solitary life in peace."

"Very poetic. And what 'feelings' did we have then?"

"Bad ones," I say. "We had bad feelings, like we had totally invaded his privacy for no reason besides our crazy adventure fantasies."

I let Fi take me down this scoldy line of questioning on purpose. For one thing, I know she likes playing the older sister like this. Plus, I *did* make this phone call to her in order to get a reality check, so there's that, too.

But I also just went with it because I like to remember times like those. They mattered. We did things that were important to us, just like Wanda is important to me now. And that gives me more resolve, not less.

"Listen, Fi. I know what you're saying," I say. "But still. If something *did* happen, I would want to do something about it, wouldn't you? And I *would* do something about it. Wouldn't you?"

Fi is quiet, and I assume she's put the phone down to deal with the kids or something. But no. She's been on the line the whole time.

"You're not going to let this go, are you?" she says, breaking the silence.

"Mrrph," I say.

Fi laughs at our running joke-noise answer: when you know what the *right* answer is but you don't want to actually give that answer, you just say 'mrrph' as a way of avoiding an answer completely.

"Alright," she says. "At least keep me posted."

"Of course," I say. "How could I have a crazy, mixed-up, 'all in my own wild imagination' adventure without you, Sis?"

"Good night, Sis."

"Night-night."

By this time, Cottage Street is definitely darker, and things seem quiet at both Wanda's and the discount store, at least from this angle.

I sit in the easy chair, reading *The Wayward Daughter*. Normally, I'd be further along in a book like this by now, but I keep putting it down every twelve minutes to look out the window.

The street lamps on either side of the block across the street make the signs have shadows like arrows, pointing towards Dollar Discount. It's like all of downtown Teabridge is pointing an accusing finger at Dollar Discount.

And if this were an Alfred Hitchcock movie, that alone would be proof that something's going on down there.

But this isn't a movie. And yes, Fi, that's disappointing.

I fall asleep in the chair again for the second night in a row, with the book in my lap.

I dream of Fi and me at the lake house. Writing each other lemon-juice-invisible-ink messages, searching the deep water for shipwrecks, and digging tunnels in the dirt to make secret passageways that no one knows about but us.

Part Four: There's Always a Thursday

Wanda paused a moment. This was the vital question, and she'd been waiting until just the right moment to ask it.

She caught his eye, held it a moment, and said, "Do you think I could send my niece a message, maybe?"

"A message?" Nate said.

"Yes. Just a simple email to let her know I'm okay. What would you think about that?"

"Oh," he said. Troubled. "I mean, it would be fine with me. But… the others. I mean, if they found out…"

"Well, I'm certainly not going to tell them," Wanda said. "You know that, right? You know that if I promise not to tell them, then I won't?"

"Yes. I do."

"Thank you," she said. "I'm glad you trust me. That means something to me. So, if it helps, you could even read the message before I send it, if you like. Just to make sure."

"That might work…" he said.

She could tell he was warming up to the idea. But she still needed to bring him along a little more. To guide him, even.

"We could do it on your laptop - the one you use for your video games," she said. "That's what you do on it, am I right? Play video games?"

He nodded.

"I figured as much," she said. "You spend so much time with it, I figured you were either playing a video game or taking an online class with the community college over in Leighton. Unless you're doing that, too?"

He shook his head, 'no.'

"But you do have that laptop with you."

He nodded.

She leaned toward him as much as she could, which is not easy when you're tied to a chair. But she wanted to be closer to him, so that she could talk in a low voice. A soothing voice.

"Why don't you go get it, huh?" she said. "What do you think?"

He reached into his duffle bag, and he pulled out his laptop.

Then he unraveled the rope from her right hand. "I probably shouldn't do more than this, because..."

"Because of the others," she said. "I know. And I understand. One hand is fine."

She balanced the laptop on one knee and opened it with her free hand.

She clicked away, making sure to say something nice to him every minute or so - like, "It's so kind of you to help me this way," or, "She's going to be so pleased to hear from me." He was afraid of the others, and she needed to keep that fear settled until she finished the message.

And... yes. Done.

"Do you want to see it, Sweetheart?" she said.

He leaned toward the laptop, scanned the message quickly, and then shrugged.

She hit 'send.'

And she waited one, two, and then three very long seconds until finally the 'message sent' notification appeared on the screen. She let out a controlled breath.

Then she noticed how quiet Nate had become. She looked closer and noticed he had a pleasant look on his face. Almost a smile, even.

"Yes, Sweetheart?" she said. "Is there something you want to say?"

"No, it's nothing," he said. "I mean, I just think it's a funny coincidence what you said about the online classes. Because I've been thinking lately about maybe going back to school."

"Have you?"

He smiled - an expression so much different than the defeated, surrendering look he had when Griff barked an order at him.

"Why don't you tell me those thoughts?" she said. "After all, we have all night, don't we?"

Toast-Log

The next thing I know, I've just opened my eyes, and I'm staring at the lace curtains.

Is it nighttime? I can't tell.

I mean, it's definitely dark outside. I think so, anyway, but I can't really see out there because the reading lamp is still on from when I fell asleep last night in the middle of a chapter.

So I turn the lamp off, and everything in the room turns into pre-dawn shadows: the couch, the coat-tree, and the oak round top table and chairs. They all become dark masses. And that makes the whole apartment feel quieter, somehow - quiet enough that I hear the low chuffle of an old engine coming from outside.

I peek through the narrow opening between the curtains, out to the street below.

It's a dark morning. Unusually dark. Weirdly dark with thick, low clouds. The glow from the street lamps has an electric feel to it. Thunder is imminent.

Yesterday morning, I had fun pretending that the street below is a heath. Now it actually feels like one.

And as I look up and down this heath, I see that there's a van in front of the discount store - the plain old rusty white van with tinted windows again. It's just sitting there with its running lights on, engine chirring away. But I can't see who's in there - not at this hour.

Finally the mysterious driver kills the engine.

Then the van just sits for a while.

So *I* sit for a while. Five minutes. Ten minutes. Twenty. Twenty-five.

I check the time. 4:50.

If this were a normal day, Wanda would turn the lights on in her shop any minute now, ready to start baking for the day.

I wait another ten minutes, but she doesn't come. No

lights. No nothing. No Wanda - which increases my suspicion even higher than it was.

And I know this isn't the main point here, but no Wanda means no muffin - which leaves me with no breakfast. And I'm hungry.

I go into my kitchenette and I put the coffee on while I make toast. On an average day, if you suggested that I have toast instead of a muffin, I'd probably say, 'sure.' I'd adjust. I'd deal with it. So why does the fact that I *can't* have a muffin this morning make me really want one, to the point where I'm actually sad? Well, you know what? What do you do when you're having toast but you really want a muffin?

You make the toast, but you find a way to make it special somehow.

You muffin-ize the toast.

So. First I toast the bread, like usual, and then I put butter and blueberry jam on it. Then I roll up each piece into a mini Yule log. And okay, a Yule log is not technically a muffin. But it is pretty special, you have to admit. And hey, you know what? I could even sprinkle some confectioners' sugar on top of it, which would really make it like a Yule log.

Because why not?

I take out the confectioners' sugar, grab a pinch, and sprinkle it over each log. The sweet dust gets on the plate. It gets on my pajamas. It gets everywhere.

And isn't that just what we love about confectioners' sugar?

I bring the plate and my mug over to the easy chair.

I take a bite, and the powdered sugar catches in my throat, of course. I cough and take a too-big sip of tea, which is still hot, and - ouch - my tongue and lips burn. I cough again and start to get back up out of the easy chair to get some ice water. Then I look down.

The van is still there, turned off. But... what's this? It looks like the note is now gone from the front door of the muffin shop. I pick up my binoculars to confirm, and yes - the note is gone. When did that happen? I'm sure it was still there when I first woke up a half hour ago.

Did it just disappear while I made my Yule log toast? It must have.

So this is good news, right? Wanda has returned? She's there now?

No. Still no lights on in the shop.

And despite the coming dawn, the sky hasn't actually gotten much lighter. It's just gotten stormier. This is going to be a total blue-black morning. I can just feel it.

And I feel it even more when Griff steps out of the front door of the discount store. Immediately, the van driver starts the engine loudly. Griff looks at the vehicle and swipes his hand urgently through the air three times, to tell the driver to pull around to the back of the building. But the driver interprets this as a 'cut the noise' gesture instead, and now the engine shuts off completely. Again.

I stick my head further through the curtains. A bit of a risk, maybe, but if Griff and his boys didn't already notice me up here with the light on all night, I doubt they'll look up here now to search the shadows for my face.

Griff approaches the driver's window, just like last night. He talks to the driver, and then the van's engine fires back up one more time with a nasty screech. Griff, clearly frustrated by the noise, looks up and down the street to see if anyone's around to notice. Apparently not.

Then he points again toward the alley that leads to the rear parking lot. The van driver finally understands what Griff is trying to tell him. He pulls up and then disappears around the corner, and Griff slips back in through the front door of the discount shop - I'm guessing to cut through the building and meet the van driver around back.

What are they doing?

I have to find out. I have to sneak down there. Now.

But I can't go yet, because I'm still in my blue-stripe pajamas. And the problem is not that they're pajamas, because obviously I've already proven to myself I have no shame about wearing them pretty much anywhere. The problem is that they are so bright I'd look like a ghost or something. A ghost who sells ice cream, maybe. But I don't have time to change, so I just need to grab something now - something that will cover me up quickly.

SuperFuzz.

I wrap it around myself, and I run out the door of my apartment, down the stairs, through the security door, and into the foyer with the dusty mailboxes. I grasp the final door handle. My thumb is on the tab. I look through the window, up and down the street as far as I can each way, especially in the direction of the alley where I'm headed. What I'm about to do is risky. No doubt about it. Because if I go through this door, I'll be officially outside. Exposed. Vulnerable, even.

I take a breath, to settle.

I press my thumb down and open the door slowly, quietly.

I step onto the sidewalk and then turn back to hold the door's outside handle - thumb pressed down on this side's tab now so that when I close it, it doesn't even click. Done. Good.

I turn around to face the street again. And now…

Time to move.

I dash across, with SuperFuzz floating up and flying behind me in the breeze from my running. I head towards the alley, keeping one eye on the front door of the discount store the whole time. The window stays dark, and the door stays closed. Good.

At the corner of the alley I stop and peak around.

The narrow passage is empty. Good again. Is anyone coming? No, I don't think so, though I do hear some faint noises from all the way around back. I scurry to the next corner, and I stop again. I hear the low rumble of the van's engine in the rear parking lot, and I sense movement. Peeking around this corner will be the riskiest thing I've done so far, but something's going on back there, and this is what I came here to do. So…

I do it. I peek.

And the first thing I see is the dumpster, which is right nearby. And that's perfect - and lucky - because it gives me some cover. I crouch down and tuck myself in behind it, and then I crab-walk to the far end and lean my head so I can see around it.

The old van is, in fact, parked near the building. Its side door is open and facing the rear door of one of the shops.

I count all the rear doors, starting at the far end: Valley Tile and Flooring, Wanda's, the discount store, Leighton Cooperative Bank, and Teabridge Financial.

That means, if I'm counting right, that the van has backed up to the door of the discount store. But Griff is standing near the next door over, which is the door of... Wanda's?

I can't tell, because I'm crouched back here. And I don't want to let my imagination get ahead of me - which, okay, has pretty much already happened, but still. But wait. Now I see Cory emerge through the door that's closer to me, which really must be the door to the discount store. But if that's true, why is Griff standing near the other one? If that's Wanda's shop, then the odds just went up that this isn't some crazy fantasy of mine. It could be the real thing.

The next weird surprise comes right away when Nate, the young one, emerges halfway *out* of the 'Griff' door. He's carrying a plain brown box about as big as a hatbox. But it's plain and brown, not with those stripy decorations or anything like they have on the hatboxes in old movies.

Cory meets him and takes the box from him. He walks to the back of the van and puts it in there, while Griff stands sentry, supervising them.

And then, thirty seconds later, they do all that again, this time with a larger, heavier box. As Nate passes it on, he catches his toe and stumbles forward, almost falling down completely, but Griff grabs his arm to help him stay upright.

Actually, 'help' is a generous word, because what Griff really does is yank him up, the way a fed-up parent pulls a pouting child up from the ground. And as Griff helps Nate get himself back together, Cory shakes his head in frustration at the clumsiness.

Personally, I have sympathy for Nate. Because I'd never join a criminal gang, obviously, but I'm pretty sure that if I *did* join one, I'd be the 'Nate.'

They load more boxes the same way, in and out, for about five minutes - which, when you're watching it happen while crouched behind a dumpster, feels like an hour.

Finally Cory gets into the van and the engine screeches into action, blowing exhaust right at me. Ugh. I didn't notice until now that I'm right next to the tailpipe.

And, wow, they really need quieter get-away cars if they're going to sneak around at dawn like this.

Cory swings the van all the way around in the parking lot. And that's bad news for me, because now I'm more exposed than I thought I'd be - and from two directions at once: Griff on one side, and Cory on the other as he pulls around the corner, right past me. So I crouch even deeper into the shadows, pulling SuperFuzz up around my head.

I stay down until the van is gone. And now that I have only one angle to worry about, I emerge from my SuperFuzz cocoon, and I peek around the dumpster.

Debris covers the ground where the van had been sitting: scraps of wood, bottles, and junk food wrappers.

Griff gathers up some of the loose material around him and brings it over to the dumpster. Yes, this dumpster - the one I'm hiding behind. I'm leaning against the back of it, and it rattles and shakes as he opens the lid and tosses some of the boards and boxes inside. The clang of the debris landing in the empty dumpster rings in my ears. And by the way, those bottles are obviously recyclable, so he really shouldn't be putting them into the regular trash. But isn't it just like a criminal to not be environmentally-minded?

He brings a little more of the debris over to the dumpster and tosses it in. I'm prepared this time, and I lean away and block my ears.

What I really need to do is get out of here and get back to my apartment. But I've lost sight of Griff, so I can't tell whether it's safe or not. I take a chance and lean even further around. And in doing so, I knock over a bottle that I didn't even know was here. It clangs when it first falls - and then rattles and pings all the way under the dumpster, beyond my reach.

Griff steps back into view as he looks for the source of the sound, and then he starts walking toward me. Directly toward me. I crouch deeper, smaller, but if he comes much closer, this crouching won't do me a bit of good.

Should I run? No. Too risky. For one thing, I don't know how fast he is. And for another thing, I'm wearing slippers - which, by the way, I can't bear to think how dirty my poor slippers are getting back here.

Should I kick him in the knee, self-defense style, before he even knows what hit him? Well, for one thing, there's the slipper thing again. I'd break my own toes. And for another thing, I couldn't really call it 'self-defense' if I attack him, out of the blue and technically unprovoked, just because I have 'a bad feeling about him.'

I mean, after all, I'm the one who's spying. He's just taking out the trash. Or at least that's how the police would hear it.

But I have to do something soon, because he's three steps away from me. Now two. And if he takes one more he'll be right here and...

Bam!

Nate bursts through the second door. What?

"Boss!" he says. "Hey, Boss!"

Griff turns and walks towards him, and Nate runs to close the gap. When they meet in the middle, Nate whispers something and Griff recoils. Then he grabs Nate by the sleeve and they slip into the first door, which I'm now sure is the discount store.

Okay, so what interrupted their attention and saved me,

right when I was about to be caught, for sure?

The answer comes as a shadow appears in the window of the second doorway. Wanda's shop.

The shadow is… a dark face.

And it's looking in my direction.

Track Team

Actually it's doing more than just look in my direction. It's looking at me.

Directly, intently at me.

Whoa.

Now it's *really* time to get out of here.

I leap from my crouch and run, kicking and stumbling until I finally emerge into the alley and dash along the side of the building towards Cottage Street, with SuperFuzz flying even higher up behind me.

And just when I get within five feet of the street, someone steps around the corner and I stop short. Whoa again.

It's a young woman. Maybe twenty years old. Dark skin, as dark as Wanda's. She faces me, looking right at me, holding a rolling pin. Is she going to hit me with it? No. I won't let her. I will not be defeated by a rolling pin!

I shoot my left foot forward and I lower my stance into a full defensive posture, preparing to respond to her attack.

I'm fired up. I'm ready.

Except, well, two things:

First of all, she's wearing an apron - which, I have to admit, makes the rolling pin look a lot less like a weapon and a lot more like… a rolling pin.

And second of all, the expression on her face is not hostile. It's not mean. And it's certainly not menacing.

It's curious. And the more she stares at me, the more familiar she seems.

"Oh," she says. "I know you."

And then it hits me that I know her too: she's Wanda's niece. I remember her from when she worked here a few years ago. She's a young woman now, but back then she was a carefree girl of seventeen or eighteen, staying with her aunt for the summer to save up money for college by working at the shop.

"Nelly?" I say. When she nods and smiles, I see a little of that girl she was back then.

I relax my combative stance, because this is not a person I need to be afraid of.

"You come into the shop every morning, right?" she says.

Now it's my turn to nod.

So we stand here, smiling and nodding, until Nelly says, "What were you doing behind the dumpster? Do you… live back there?"

"What?" I say. "Why would you ask that?" But, of course, I'm standing here in my pajamas, clutching SuperFuzz. And I *was*, just now, crouched behind the dumpster. So I guess that's a fair question, worth answering.

"No," I say. "I live in an apartment nearby."

"Then what were you doing back there? I mean, if you don't mind me asking."

I don't know how to say it, except to just say it. "I was spying on your neighbors."

"Oh," she says, like that's a perfectly normal answer. Then she realizes that it isn't. "Wait, you were *spying*?"

"Yeah. On those three guys from the discount store."

"Is that who was making all that noise?"

"Yes!" I say. "Did you see them? Have you had any contact with them?"

"I haven't had contact with anyone," she says. "I just got here, maybe ten minutes ago. But what are they doing that makes you want to spy on them?"

"I don't know what they're doing," I say. "But it's not good, whatever it is."

"Hm," she says. "This is very strange, I have to say. Where's Wanda?"

"I was just going to ask you the same question."

A drop of rain lands on Nelly's shoulder. She looks up at the sky. Then a drop lands on my shoulder, and we both look up at the sky.

"Can we go inside?" she says. "All the sudden it feels weird to be out here, for some reason."

"I know that feeling well," I say. "Is the front door of Wanda's place open?"

"Yeah. I unlocked it when I got here," she says. "I still have my own key from a few years ago."

She starts to walk back around the corner, right out into the open, so I grab her sleeve.

"Wait," I say. "Stop."

She winces a little, and I realize that, in my mild panic, I grabbed her a little too hard. "I'm sorry," I say. "But we have to be careful. I don't want them to see us."

"So… you want us to…?"

"Stay down," I say. "And stay close to the building, at least until we find out if they're in the empty shop."

"Um…" she says. Obviously I haven't completely won her over to my crazy spy caper yet, and that's fair enough. So, yet again, the only way to say it is to say it.

"Listen," I tell her. "Honestly, I don't know what's going on here, and I don't even definitely know if anything *is* going on. But I haven't seen your Aunt Wanda for a few days now, and I'm really starting to get worried. And now you don't know where she is either, right?"

"No, I don't. But, like I say, I only just got h-"

"Yeah, but I'm not talking about just today," I interrupt. "Have you talked to her in the last few days? Heard from her or anything?"

"Well, no. But…"

"Alright, then," I say. "I mean, I know this is weird, but can we, like, sneak back into your aunt's shop so we can talk about this? I promise I'll tell you everything I know once we get into the shop."

"Okay, fine," she says. "If it's that important to you, I'll do it. But how do we 'sneak' in through the front door of a shop on a main street?"

"Like this," I say. She follows me as we creep along the

front side of Bank Row, staying low and tight to the building. We get past Teabridge Financial and the bank, which are two places that are always quiet this early in the morning.

But next up is the discount store, and I already know that's not quiet. I got lucky just a few minutes ago, when Nelly distracted Griff at the very moment he was about to find me behind the dumpster, but I'm not going to press that luck.

So, now that the discount store guys have taken the newspapers down from the window, how do we get to Wanda's shop without them seeing us?

We could do a big reverse around the whole block, and then approach Wanda's from the other direction. That worked well enough yesterday afternoon after I finished talking to Devin.

But the rain is really starting to fall now, and it's still dark. If anything, it's gotten darker in the last few minutes. The full walk around the block now seems far too long and far too gloomy.

So… forward, I say. Now, voyager.

At the edge of the discount store's window, I lean out slowly, inch by inch, until I can see most of the inside of the store's showroom.

"It looks dark," I tell Nelly. "To me it does, anyway. They must be in the back or something. Take a look."

Nelly joins me in leaning out. Through the window, we see the dim shadows of the tables in the middle with their makeshift display boxes, and we see the temporary shelves along the wall. But no Griff. No Cory. No Nate.

"Does it look safe to you?" I ask her.

"I *guess*," she whispers.

"Me too," I say. "But they could come out at any point. So sneak past. But do it quickly."

She starts to speak: "Do you really think we need to…?" But she stops herself, mid-question, when she sees the look on my face.

"Okay, fine. I'll sneak past," she says. "But how does a

person 'sneak *quickly*'? It's like if someone said, 'murmur loudly.' The words don't quite go together."

"How about a dash, then?" I say. "You can dash, can't you?"

"Now you're talking," she says. "Watch this." She lowers down into a sprinter's starting position, which reminds me that she actually *was* a sprinter in high school. Back during that summer when she worked here, she went for runs in the early afternoons after she finished at the shop. And her steady, powerful crouch tells me she hasn't lost the form in the few years since then.

"Fire when ready," I say.

She takes a breath, and then she goes: she dashes until she gets to Wanda's door. It takes only three seconds, total. Maybe less, if that's even possible.

When she's safely out of view of the window, she spins around in place to face me. We both pause a moment, to see if it worked. Did they notice her?

No lights go on. No one comes out. We don't hear any noises.

She got past okay.

My turn.

I lower down into the same sprinter position Nelly used, because it seemed to help her go so fast. The problem is, I never was a sprinter - not in high school nor at any other time in my life. So for me, it just makes me more clumsy. If *that's* even possible.

Oh, well. No turning back now.

I pull SuperFuzz back over my head again like a hood, and I look down, so that all I can see through the hood-hole is the cobblestones of the sidewalk. And, wow, even in this tense, uncertain situation, I feel a moment of comfort that makes me want to stay under here and just block out the world entirely.

But Nelly must sense my hesitation, because before I completely talk myself out of going, I hear her whisper to me: "Ready?"

I nod my head, still under the blanket.

She starts a countdown. "Three… two… one…"

At 'one,' I go.

I scoot across like a sped-up turtle, with SuperFuzz as my shell. My head is down the whole time. Cobblestone after cobblestone passes through my small oval field of vision until I feel a friendly tug on my arm as Nelly pulls me up and into the doorway of the muffin shop. We stumble in through the door, tripping over SuperFuzz on the way. I scramble back up and lock the front door.

Done. We're in.

I take a breath and look around the place.

The lights are off. It's dim, and quiet, and a little spooky. But also, somehow, comforting at the same time.

"So what's going on h-" Nelly starts to say.

But I cut her off. "Wait. Listen."

We wait. We listen.

It might just be the rain outside, but I think I hear faint noises from the back.

We walk through the shop into the kitchen area, past the prep counter and the pans and the baking ovens. It's pretty neat being back here, actually, and I'd like to poke around. But there's business at hand, so I stay focused.

At the far end of the kitchen is the door to the basement. It's wooden with panels, like a bedroom door. I open it, and we step onto the landing at the top of the stairs. The deeper the stairs go, the darker and quieter they get. It certainly doesn't seem like anyone's down there.

"You haven't been downstairs yet this morning, right?" I ask Nelly.

She shakes her head. Then she calls out, "Wanda?" so suddenly that she not only startles me, she actually startles herself.

"Sorry about that," she whispers. "That really echoes."

We wait for a response.

Nothing.

All seems quiet. All seems secure.

So we go back to the front of the shop.

I double-check that I definitely locked the front door. I did.

Okay.

Finally.

We sit on the couch - sideways, facing each other.

"Hi," I say.

"Yeah, hi," she says, laughing. "Can I just say that this is really fun - what we're doing. But... what *are* we doing? Because I know that, okay, Wanda hasn't shown up for work yet today. But it's still early, isn't it?"

"Not really. Not by Wanda's standards."

"Okay," she says. "But she'll be here soon, right?"

"I certainly hope so," I say. "I'd love to find out everything is fine around here."

"Either way, this is definitely not how I expected my first morning back at the job to be like."

"So that's why you've come here? To work?"

"Yes, for the summer. Or maybe longer. I don't know. I just got my associates degree," she says. And then she pauses and looks at me, expectantly.

"Oh, right," I say. "Congratulations. That's awesome."

"Thank you. I'm very proud of myself, as you can obviously tell. Anyway, I wanted a break before I go back for a bachelor's, so I asked my aunt if I could come here. And she said 'yes.' Of course."

"When did you ask her?"

"Earlier this week. Tuesday, I think," Nelly says. "Yes, I sent her an email on Tuesday afternoon."

"Two days ago."

She nods.

"Okay," I say. "That explains why she didn't tell me on Tuesday morning that you were coming."

"It was definitely spontaneous on my part, but if I'm going to work in some retail store for the summer, I'd much rather do it at Aunt Wanda's than anywhere else. And she emailed back and said, 'Sure. Come any time.'"

"And that's it? One email, and then you come?"

"That's all I need with Aunt Wanda," she says. "I mean, not to take my aunt for granted, but if I hadn't written to her at all and just showed up one morning out of the blue, she would have handed me an apron like it was nothing. Because that's just like her, isn't it?"

"Yes," I say. "That's just like Wanda."

"So after she emailed me with a 'yes,' I packed my bags and filled up my car with gas, just like I did a few summers ago. We knew the routine, you know? Didn't need to say much more to each other. But now I kind of wish I *had* actually talked to her because… are you telling me something has happened to her?"

It's her first flash of real concern. And that makes *me* concerned all the sudden. Have I made too much of this? Is this all just a crazy adventure fantasy, like my sister and I used to have at the lake house?

It's one thing for me to concoct a whole story just to amuse Fi while she does the dishes. That's harmless fun. But to tell this whole crazy story to Nelly, a family member, without actually knowing that anything has gone wrong at all? Well, that suddenly seems irresponsible. Why didn't I think of all this before? Why am I coming to my senses only now? I don't know. But there's no time like the present to start making sense.

So I back off.

"No," I say. "I have no actual reason to think anything has happened to Wanda," I say. "I want to be very clear about that, because I don't want to freak you out."

"Well, you're kind of freaking me out anyway," she says. "But thank you for that reassurance. Except you said you had no *actual* reason for thinking anything has happened. What's your 'un-actual' reason?"

I don't want to tell her. And she can tell by the look on my face that I don't want to tell her.

Which of course makes her want to hear it even more.

"You have to say it at this point," she says. "Hiding behind dumpsters. Sneaking around windows. Locking doors. You have to explain all this."

"Alright, fine," I say. "I'm concerned because, the last time either of us saw her or heard from her was Tuesday morning. And then these guys show up and open this discount store all the sudden. It just seemed mysterious. And then last night, that note on the door appeared. I know this isn't definite or tangible. But..."

"It's okay," she says. "I appreciate that you're concerned for my Aunt. But there's a simple solution to this: I'll just call her."

She takes out her phone and presses the icon for her aunt - which is a picture of a gray cat. The call goes to voicemail, so she leaves a message: "Hi Aunt Wanda, it's Nell. I'm at the shop. Wondering where you are. Please check in."

Then she looks up at me. "How does that sound?"

"Nice," I say. "Concerned but not alarmed."

She sends the same message in a text and an email, along with a bunch of heart and love emojis at the end of each one, of course.

She clicks her phone off. Done.

"Good," I say. "Alright. And by the way, did you stop by her house when you got to town?"

"No - I haven't stopped by anywhere yet. I pretty much got off the interstate at five-thirty this morning and drove straight here. Now that I think about it, I *would* like to go to her house to see if she's okay, but I don't want to leave the shop at this point either. The last thing I told her in my email from Tuesday was that I'd be up and ready for work today. For all we know, she's just doing some early errands because she's counting on me to open up for her on time."

"Okay, so..." I say. "I could go to her house, if you want me to. She lives on the west side, right? That's on my way into work. If you tell me her address, I'll stop by. If you're okay with that, I mean. I realize that we only kind of know each other, and that it might be weird."

"The whole thing is weird already," she says. "And I guess if you were some crazy criminal who's after Wanda, you could find her on the internet whether I tell you now or not. So..."

She shows me Wanda's contact info on her phone: 18 Cloverdale Drive.

"Thank you," I say. "When I go there, I won't go inside or anything. I'll just ring and see if she answers. And if she doesn't, at least we'll know if the house is fine and everything. I mean, it probably will be."

"Right. Probably," she says. "But it would be nice to know that for sure."

"Exactly.'

"Good. Right," she says. "No big deal, right? We're just making sure."

"And for what it's worth, I don't leave for work until eight-thirty, so there's still time for this whole thing to just work out on its own, with Wanda showing up after all."

"In the meantime I'm going to open the shop, for Wanda's sake," Nelly says. "It's her livelihood, after all."

"I can help you, if you want," I say. "The only thing I wanted to do this morning before work was to read this mystery novel I've been into, and..."

"You're telling me we've got a real-life mystery novel going on right here," Nelly says.

"That's what I'm telling you."

She throws me an apron, which I need because I *am* still wearing my pajamas. "Where do we start?" I ask her.

"Alright," she says. "When I worked here two years ago, blueberry muffins were my specialty. And I already checked the fridge. Plenty of blueberries in there. If I focus on those, I'll be offering just one kind of fresh-baked muffin to start with, and then Wanda can make more when she gets here. Because she *is* going to get here, right?"

"Yeah," I say, to encourage her optimism. "Sure she will."

"Right. And so the blueberry muffins and the day-olds and lots of coffee should keep things going until she does."

"Sounds good," I say.

Nelly works on mixing the muffin batter while I set everything else up: I turn on the lights and start the coffee, I put all the remaining baked goods on special, and I arrange the furniture.

She directs me through all this, looking up through the square space in the dividing wall between the kitchen and the seating area. She gives good instructions: clear and direct. Just as I finish one task, she leads me to the next.

"You say you don't remember much about working here a few summers ago," I say, "but it seems like you really know what you're doing."

"It's in my blood, I guess," she says. "Do you know that I kind of grew up with Aunt Wanda?"

"You visited her a lot?"

"Yes. But it was even more than that. My Mom was sick for a while when I was young - like nine years old? Something like that. They sent me to live with Wanda during the summer, to get me out of the way while my Mom tried to get better. Unfortunately it didn't work, though."

"You mean it didn't work to get you out of the way?" I ask. "Or it didn't work for your Mom to get better?"

She frowns. And now that I think about it, I remember Wanda mentioning once that she had a sister who died young.

"Oh," I say. "I'm so sorry."

"Thanks," she says. "It's been a while, which helps. And good things can come from sad things, because they help you appreciate the people you still have in your life, you know?"

I nod.

"Is your Mom still alive?" she asks me.

"Yes, but I don't see her much," I say. "My parents got divorced when I was little, and my Mom said she needed time to herself to work some things out. That's pretty much the last we saw of her. It's complicated, obviously. But it's okay. My older sister Fiona took care of me. Still does, to be perfectly honest with you. We became really close as a result, so I suppose that's my good thing that came from a sad thing."

"Fiona is your Aunt Wanda?"

"Yeah," I say, nodding. "I guess you're right."

Chatting like this while we work helps. It calms us, settles us.

It settles me, anyway. Nelly's been calm the whole time. I think my nuttiness amuses her.

And if it does, I'm glad.

Less than an hour later, the shop is open. A few regular customers are nestled around the cafe tables, happily enjoying their deep-discount baked goods. Coffee is flowing, and the air is filled with the smell of Nelly's blueberry muffins, which are now ready to come out of the oven.

There's still plenty more work for Nelly to do, but at least we've made a good start together.

"I should go," I tell her. "Though I don't feel incredibly comfortable leaving you alone here when I'm gone."

She can't stifle a laugh at my concern. "I'm sorry to laugh," Nelly says. "You're very sweet. But I'll be fine, obviously. And if it helps you, I promise to leave the back door double-locked, and I'll add the security bar. I won't even go into the basement for supplies, because the only thing I remember how to bake is more of these blueberry muffins, and we have everything we need for those right here. I'll be up here at the counter helping customers, or baking in the kitchen. Either way, I'll have a full view of the front window the whole time. Is that good? Will that ease your mind?"

"I guess," I say. "But let's also text each other, to check in."

She shrugs a 'sure' and we exchange numbers.

"Alright, I'm leaving now," I say. "Wow, you're so brave about all this. Braver than I would be."

"You're kidding, right?" she says. And I laugh, because I assume she's joking. But she's not laughing at me. She's smiling.

Did I just miss a compliment? Was she trying to say that I'm brave? Oh, well. It wouldn't be the first one I've missed in my lifetime, that's for sure. And I have other things to worry about, like how to get back across the street.

In my pajamas.

With a comforter draped over my shoulders.

And that's going to look weird and probably suspicious to anyone who sees me. It's not so dark out anymore, either, and the street is no longer empty. No way to hide.

"Feel free to keep the apron on, if that helps," Nelly says.

"Thanks," I say. "But will it be enough? The apron covers only the front of me. Outside on the street, people will see me from all sides."

I step out from behind the counter and slowly turn around, to give her the full view.

"Be honest," I say. "Now that you see the whole 'me,' does the apron make me look less crazy or *more* crazy?"

"Oh," she says. "I see your point. Your outfit is a bit busy, to say the least. Why not leave your comforter here? That might help."

I look at her like now *she's* the one who's crazy. Leave SuperFuzz behind? I clutch my fleecy friend. "We've been through too much together for us to part now."

"Fair enough," she says. "Then you know what? Here's what you should do: just walk across the street, just as you are, and don't care what anyone thinks or says. They'll probably just assume we've had some weird adult slumber party or something, complete with blankies."

"Yeah?" I say. And I know it's beside the point, but how weird is it that an adult slumber party, complete with blankies, sounds like a total blast to me?

"Alright," I say. "Here goes."

I step out front, into the rainy morning. This time, I don't use SuperFuzz like a shawl. Instead, I wrap one end around my neck like a superhero cape. Three years ago, when I first bought this blanket and decided to call it SuperFuzz, I had no idea how appropriate the name would be.

That could be my superhero name, actually: *I am SuperFuzz. I have come to restore the order of Teabridge.*

I take a breath, and I dash across the street, my cape flapping behind. When I finally slip into the vestibule of my building, I stop for another breath, as SuperFuzz settles around me. I stand right in the window of the front door, and I look down the street once more at the shops and the old-fashioned lamplight-style street lights.

Above all that is the dawning day. The sun is fighting its way through the rain clouds over the mountains of the Edicom Valley.

I look back one more time at Wanda's shop, through the window where a customer stands at the counter, trying to decide what she wants. Nelly pretends she has to rearrange the trays of muffins in the display case, but I can tell that what she's really doing is watching me, just like she was watching me as I crossed the street a moment ago.

And maybe she's just trying to figure out if I'm some completely loopy person, so I nod to her to let her know that, whether I'm loopy or not, if her Aunt Wanda's in trouble, I'll help her. I won't give up. I'll find a way.

Does it work? Does a simple expression on my face convey all this through the rain-streaked window - all the way across the street and then through another rain-streaked window?

No, I think. No way, right?

Except for one thing: she nods right back.

Small Choices, Deliberately

Up in my apartment, I take a shower and then go into my bedroom to get dressed.

And do I want to put my pajamas back on and just stay home, staked out with my binoculars at the window, all while thinking of more new ways to turn toast into different kinds of pastry?

Yes. I do want to do that.

And you know what? Maybe I *should* do that. After all, it's been well-established that TechTile isn't a nine-to-five kind of place. Ashley even said that outright at yesterday's meeting in her speech about moving 'beyond the hours-of-the-day and days-of-the week paradigm.' And I know I should welcome that approach, because it would allow me to stay home more. I've always said my ideal life is all day sitting in an easy chair, wearing the clothes I slept in.

The truth is, I'm too set in my ways to change my work habits that much all at once, but maybe I could at least leave work early this afternoon. I could tell Jannelle I'm taking work home with me, which would also give me a chance to keep an eye on Nelly.

I get dressed and carry my bags down to the foyer, and then I stop and survey the street through the window in the front door. In Wanda's shop, a few more people sit at the cafe tables in the window, and Nelly works away inside. Good.

Outside the discount store, Devin is setting up for another day of work. I watch him take his ladder off the van's roof-rack. He hops onto the running board and unhooks the ratchet straps. The ladder tilts and falls off the roof towards his head, but he hops back down and catches it just as it finishes its first half-turn. I'm impressed by the casual way he holds the long, heavy ladder in one hand as he surveys the sidewalk, choosing the best way to set up. I like a worker who makes each small choice deliberately.

I'm starting to like a lot about him, actually.

He's come so far since eleventh grade when I tutored him in Physics. I remember a moment in our classroom after school: he and I alone with the clacking balls and the posters of the solar system. We sat at one of the long black stone counters in the big echoey room that's usually so full and busy, working on an "Everyday Physics in Action" word problem which asked how long a cup rolling off a table would take to land on the floor. It involved these complicated formulas for the force you used to knock it over and the friction of the table when it rolled, and… well, a lot more that I've long forgotten.

I remember pausing in the middle of trying to explain the problem to Devin, and he just wasn't getting it. And I bet that if they had just given him an actual cup and a table, he could have figured out the problem in a snap. And not just by timing it with his cellphone. I'm saying if he actually had the objects in hand, he probably could have figured out the physics equations, too. There were two things missing from the "Everyday Physics in Action" problem: the 'everyday' and the 'action.'

But now, after struggling in school, he's found his groove. And I see what he's accomplished since then. I'm really glad for him - and even, I have to say, a little proud of him, because he learned a trade and even seems to be pretty good at it.

And I can see how he wouldn't like this pointless job that the discount store guys have given him - replacing trim that doesn't need to be replaced. Devin is a craftsman now, not someone content with busy work.

After thinking about him so much like this, I want to stop over and say hi to him. But I really need to get out of here, and I still don't want the discount store guys to see where I live. So I transfer all my work bags (and I have to admit, I really do have a lot of work bags) into my left hand, and I put my right hand on the door handle in the ready position. Just as two pedestrians pass by, heading to the left, I slip out the door and walk beside them, on the building side, staying hidden behind them.

I walk down several yards until I'm perpendicular to the alley, and then I cross the street - just like any normal human being would. No pajamas this time. No heath. No superhero cape.

Just me. Just your average, typical office worker on her way to work. Nothing to see here, folks.

When I get through the alley and then back to the rear lot, I walk straight to my car. My peripheral vision doesn't show me anything particularly untoward going on back here, and that's just fine with me. My only goal right now is getting safely to my car.

Which I do. Good.

Safe and sound and everything normal, right?

Well, not quite, because on my way to work, before I get to the interstate, I turn off into Wanda's neighborhood.

A Grey Tabby Named Powder

Cloverdale is one of the 'box' streets - a pleasant and quiet grid of square blocks like a checkerboard on the west side of Teabridge. I don't know it well, and it's hard for me to distinguish one street from the next. Finally I do find Cloverdale, though if you ask me to retrace my steps, I doubt I could.

I follow the numbers until I get to Wanda's place, one house in from the end of the block. It's a sweet, white Cape with black shutters and two dormers in the front. There's a small sitting porch with hanging Bougainvilleas and a white porch swing.

The windows are dark and the house itself is quiet. I open the gate in the chain-link fence. I walk up and I ring the bell. I wait. Nothing.

There's a knocker, a very old bronze one so tarnished it feels like it has a second skin. And it's heavier than it looks.

Knock. Knock. Knock.

I wait. Still nothing.

I wait some more, just to make sure, even though I can just feel that no one's here. Another minute. Two minutes.

Nobody home.

I walk around the house. All is fine on these sides, too.

I text Nelly: *She's not here. Place seems quiet, though. Nothing suspicious.*

Nelly texts back a thumbs-up emoji.

I'm about to leave the yard when a gray tabby cat comes trotting out of the bushes. It stops when it sees me, taking a moment to figure out that I'm not Wanda. But then it walks up to me anyway and brushes its shoulder against my leg. I bend down and pet it.

It has a collar with a bell and an identification tag. No name though - just an 800-number for a pet-finding service.

Is this Wanda's cat? Does she even have one? She must, because her icon on Nelly's phone is a gray cat.

I write another text to Nelly: *Does Wanda have a cat?*

When I type the word 'cat,' my phone automatically offers me a choice of emojis. My impulse is to not use one, because this isn't a game. I'm here for a serious reason.

But, wow, one of them is a big, round cat-face looking at you with glowing, smiling brown eyes. Extremely cute. And it's even a gray tabby cat like this one. So I add that one after all, of course.

Nelly texts me back: *She does have a cat. A gray tab named Powder.*

Okay. That fits what I'm seeing. To be sure, I click a photo of the cat and send it to her as well.

She texts back right away: *Powder!*

Okay, then. Powder it is.

The cat looks at me and purrs, inviting me to join her as she ducks halfway back under the bush and then drops down and rubs her back into the dirt. Thank you for the invitation, Powder, but I regret to say that I must decline.

She's very sweet, though. She certainly looks healthy enough - not neglected or abandoned, which tells me that someone has been taking care of her for the last few days. But that person doesn't have to be Wanda, because cats are pretty resourceful - begging for treats at houses around the neighborhood, and usually getting them. Plus there's surely a mouse or two in the basement of these cute old houses.

I look around some more.

There's a church the next block over. Is that the one Wanda goes to? Is there someone there I could talk to? I walk up to it. The sign out front lists Sunday services, and a Wednesday evening gathering. I think Wanda's mentioned going to church events on Wednesdays. Today is Thursday, so did Wanda go last night? Maybe I could find out.

I walk all the way up to the door, and I try the handle. It's locked. I look on either side of the church, but there doesn't seem to be a parish hall or rectory or any other associated building. Nothing to follow here.

Nothing to follow anywhere, it seems. And I'm already making myself late enough for work.

So I walk back to Wanda's house. I step inside the fence for one more lap around the yard. Powder is now fully lounging under the front bushes, amused by my movements. And her eyes are not the only ones on me right now: a neighbor across the street is standing in her living room window, looking at me. I look right back at her, and I'm about to wave. But she ducks back behind the curtain.

I feel bad, because I came here to check on Wanda, not freak out her neighbors.

So I leave.

Noon-ish

At work, I make it all the way to my cubicle without anyone noticing that it's 9:09.

I'm nine minutes late. Nine!

I drop my bags under my desk and turn on my computer. While it boots up, I go into the break room to fill my mug with tea.

Rennie from Media is here, getting a cup of coffee for herself. "Big news, huh?" she says.

She says it offhandedly yet at the same time sort of urgently, catching me off-guard to the point where I come shockingly close to saying, *Oh, I know. It's so weird that Wanda is missing. What do you think has happened to her?* - as though Wanda's disappearance could possibly be the big news she's talking about.

Fortunately I stop myself just in time. "Yeah?" I say, inviting her to continue without admitting that I don't know what she actually *is* talking about.

"The chatroom thread, of course."

"Mmm?" I say, nodding.

"Short term, things could be sticky during construction," she says. "But long term, what's good for Bradley is good for us. That's what I think, anyway."

Okay, there's my first clue: Bradley - which I'm guessing refers to Bradley airport, since that's just a half-hour southeast of us.

"Anything that opens up connections is good for a commodities broker, right?" she adds.

So I nod again, still not a hundred percent sure of what's going on. And it actually seems to work, because she smiles and says, "Well, thanks for checking in. This has been really helpful."

That's nice to hear. But *how* was I helpful? I gotta tell you,

I'm not exactly sure. So I just say, "You're very welcome. It's been helpful to me, too." And that's not a lie, because I've learned two things: one is that you can sometimes be useful to people even when you don't know what they're talking about. The other is that there's an online thread I should look at.

I go back to my desk, and I put my tea mug into its mug-sweater. I open the company chatroom to read the discussion. I guessed right a minute ago; the big news is that Bradley International Airport - 'our' airport - is planning some major renovations that will affect domestic flights in the short-term. And my fellow TechTile employees have been speculating all morning as to what this means for us.

Some are wondering whether we'll have to move the office on a temporary basis. And then others say, maybe we should take it a step further and just close the office completely and work remotely.

But if that happened, would we have a company at all?

As I finish reading, Jannelle comes over and says, "Good morning, Liz. I'm glad you're here. I heard you finished the current innovations fabric report?"

"Or future innovations, depending on how you look at it," I say. "And yes, I finished it. Sent it to Danny yesterday."

"Oh. Wow. Good. Any come-backs from him?"

"Just a few."

"Alright, then," she says. "Look at you. Laser focus."

That's funny, because it feels the only focusing I've been doing in the last two days is when I adjust my binoculars to spy on Griff and his gang.

But Jannelle is smiling, so I smile.

"Next project, then?" I say.

"You're on it already," she says, noticing that my computer is open to the chatroom. "Management wants you to take a look at some of the options we have if this Bradley thing is as big a deal as we think it's going to be. Did you see that some people are proposing moving the office?"

"Yes," I say because I did see it, exactly 7.4 seconds before

Jannelle approached me.

"What's your thinking?"

"Me?" I say. "What do I think?"

"Yeah. Seems like you have a thought."

She's right. I do have a thought. But frankly I was hoping she didn't notice, because it's not the kind of thought that she's probably looking for.

But she's staring at me, and she's expecting an answer.

So. What the heck. Here goes.

"To be honest with you, Janelle, I only looked at the thread just now. But from what I've read, I don't think we should close the branch. I just think that people like to have a place to be. They may not act like it all the time, but if you take this place away from them, they'll miss it - probably more than they realize. It's like... a muffin shop, for example."

"A muffin shop?"

"Yeah. A place you can go and sit and just relax."

"You mean a cafe?" she says.

"Well, yeah," I say. "But one that specializes in muffins."

"They still have places like that?"

"Sure. I mean, there's at least one that I know of."

"Sounds nice."

"I know, right?" I say. "You can just buy a muffin at a supermarket, or you could just make them yourself. But people want to *be* someplace, especially someplace they can go regularly. You get attached to the people you see there - the regular customers, or the woman who owns the shop. They become part of your life. And I know that saying hi to someone every morning is not the same as knowing them like you know your family, but it's still meaningful, you know?"

"Right," she says. And I assume she means it the way you say 'Right, *riiight...*" to a crazy person as you slowly back away. This makes me cringe inside so much that I can't hold it any longer, so I let the cringe spill out all over my face. And I'm about to come completely clean and say, 'Look, I work hard on the projects you give me, but obviously I'm not the one to ask about these kinds of things. So I'm sorry to take up your time with all this nonsense.''

But before I can say this, she says, "Wow. That's a really good perspective. We're all gung-ho with this 'close the office' thing, but we'll lose accounts if we don't think it through."

She means all this: it's a genuine compliment. I should feel proud and gratified, and I do. But I also feel like the guy from that old movie about the gardener who's mistaken for a political genius because all his talk of caring for plants sounds like deep wisdom for 'growing' the nation's economy.

"You're always so calm about things," she says. "It's a perspective we need to keep in touch with."

And just when I think the conversation will mercifully end, Danny from sales stops by.

"Oh, good," he says. "You're both here. Jannelle, I assume you're updating her on what we need this morning?"

"I am," she said. "And Lizzie's been sharing her perspective."

Oh, no. She's not going to tell him what I just said...

Yes. She is.

She tells him every inane thing, almost word for word. Now I am beyond cringing. I close my eyes, tight. I don't care how it looks. And in my mind I am racing across the Swedish Alps handcuffed to a dishy, mustachioed, rakish rogue, evading Nazis in our quest to deliver military secrets to the allies. When my mind-movie ends, I open my eyes.

Danny is nodding. So... he likes my ideas? Apparently.

"Will you be able to work something up this morning?" he says.

"Sure," I say. "On the feasibility of closing the office or moving it elsewhere temporarily, and the options therein, should we choose either of those routes."

"Yes. Good," he says. "But don't forget your position on keeping things just as they are. It deserves to be part of the conversation."

"I'll give a fair hearing to all sides, and I'll have something for you by lunchtime," I say.

"Great," Danny says. "Wait, what time is lunch?"

"Noon," I say, though maybe I should have said, 'Noon-ish,' just to give the impression that I don't stop to eat my lunch at exactly twelve o'clock each day. As in, one second after 11:59:59.

Danny and Jannelle leave, and I turn to my desk. I like having a clearly defined work-task to immerse into for the morning, and this is a good one - which will hopefully give me some of that focus Jannelle thinks I already have. And, who knows, maybe I can even forget about Wanda for a while?

No. That's not going to happen. Because thinking about *not* thinking about her makes me think about her. So before I jump into my project, I pull my phone out of my bag, and then slip it into my lap, so that I can text Nelly without anyone seeing me.

I type out a text: *At work now. How's it going?*

She texts back thirty second later: *Busy here at shop. Lots of weird-vibe lingering from the boys next store. But nothing definite.*

I text back: *Okay. Hope things stay quiet. Keep me posted.*

Over the next hour, while I work on my 'move vs. don't move' assessment, I don't hear anything else from Nelly. That's not surprising. After all, morning is the high-traffic time for a muffin shop.

But another hour passes, and now it's eleven o'clock. Still nothing.

That *is* surprising.

I want to text her again, but I was the last one to send a text during our earlier exchange, so how can I reinitiate without seeming too pushy?

I could go the indirect route and just forward some funny gif from the internet, like a funny cat thing. Or something with muffins, maybe - a walking muffin, or a laughing muffin, or I don't know, dancing muffins. I look it up, and it takes me only ten seconds to find three dancing muffin gif's and endless pages of cats in funny places. I could send any of these, and then all she'd have to do is respond with an LOL, and then I'd know she's alright.

But that feels dishonest, you know? I don't mean dishonest in any deep and serious way - it's just that what I want to know is if she's okay, not whether she thinks a cat sleeping in a houseplant is funny. I mean, it *is* funny, but keep your focus, Lizzie. That's the word of the day. Focus.

So I just write, *Hi. Hope you're still holding on.*

She doesn't write back. So I try again: *Are you?*

Still nothing.

I dive back into my TechTile work with nervous energy. I feel like there's a big sand timer on my desk like in *The Wizard of Oz* and I'm racing to finish the project before the last grain falls. Because you know what? If I finish by lunch and I still haven't heard from Nelly, I'm going to leave. Everyone else does it, so I will. I'll drive back to Teabridge, and I'll just go see Nelly.

At 11:50, right before lunch, I hit 'send' on the document I worked on all morning.

Danny immediately responds with a thumb's up and smiley face emoji sent from his cell phone. Those are nice emojis to get, but does that mean he's officially accepting the report? I need to know that. I can't leave until I get that official acceptance, because if he does have any come-backs, they're likely to involve soliciting people in the office for their opinion, face-to-face.

And I don't want to just sit here wondering, so I write back to him: *Feel free to send come-backs, if any.*

I basically stare back and forth at my phone and the clock for ten minutes - i.e., six hundred seconds. Nothing. I shouldn't expect any different. Danny's initial response came from his phone, not his desktop or even his laptop, which confirms that he's on the road somewhere. Which means he's barely had time to read the report, never mind work up come-backs for me.

Now it's noon, lunchtime, and still no word. You know

what? If I leave now, I could do a round trip to Cottage Street and back. It's a tight window, twenty minutes each way if there's no traffic. I could eat my lunch in the car on the way and still be back by one o'clock, right? I check the driving app on my phone, and it's a good thing I do, because the interstate is all red, which means it's totally backed up with traffic.

So that's that. I'm here at least through lunch.

I want to eat outside like usual, but it's still rainy. So I eat in the breakroom, which is okay. Not exactly a Paris cafe, though. There are no windows, it's cramped, and there are only two round tables - thick laminate ones, more like you'd find in a second grade classroom than on a rainy cobblestone street in France.

Still, it's a place where I can watch people come and go. They fill up their coffee mugs and retrieve food from the fridge. Then they take it elsewhere to eat, probably their desks.

Most people who come in don't even notice that I'm here. And that's especially strange because my head is buzzing. Do you ever notice how strange it is that your head can be filled with so many noisy, frantic thoughts, but the people around you can't hear any of them? And the buzziest, noisiest, most frantic thought I'm having right now is a question: Why hasn't Nelly gotten back to me?

Out of anxiety, I finish my lunch within twenty minutes. So with all this extra time, I go down to the lobby and out the front door and just stand under the big overhang, to look out on the misty day. Since it's too wet to sit on the bench, at least I can stand here and *see* the bench. And I can breathe the air, and even bend down and touch the grass - thick and heavy with raindrops.

So you know what? If there are no come-backs on this morning's report, I'm definitely leaving early. Yes, you heard me right: I'm leaving the office early, just so I can see Nelly. Make sure she's okay. I mean, I'm sure she is.

Right? She's okay, isn't she?

Back at my desk, I double my focus from this morning,

finishing any other odds and ends and catching up on the company chatroom stuff I missed at lunch, so that as soon as I get the word that the report has passed on to admin, nothing will hold me back.

A little before two o'clock, Jannelle swings by my cubicle.

"The final from Danny is in," she says. "He says to tell you, 'Nice work this morning.'"

"Great," I say. "Thanks. So no come-backs at all?"

"Nope. Nothing right away. He still likes your thinking on the option of staying right where we are, and he expects they'll want you to work up more on it. But the steering committee needs to review it first, and you know how long that can take."

"Okay. Sounds good," I say. "So…"

Here it comes. I'm about to ask her if I can leave early.

Ah! Can I even do this? It just feels… weird.

I mean, I *know* I *could* do it. It gets so quiet around here in the afternoons, and today is no exception. Most people don't even ask whether they can leave. They just do it. Even Jannelle and the accounting twins do it sometimes. Not very often, but sometimes.

So why not me?

What the heck. Do it. Try it. One time.

"Hey - you know what, Jannelle?" I say, trying to sound off-hand. "I'm thinking I may take off. I'll bring some stuff home with me. I won't go too far with the thing for Danny until they've mapped out a plan. But there are some things I could look at that would still be helpful."

"Oh," she says. She's nodding. She smiles a little smile, which of course I immediately assume to mean that she's laughing at me. Judging me. Mentally composing my termination notice and then signing it with a nasty flourish, using a quill-tip pen and lots of deep black ink, like the villain in a Dickens novel.

But no. None of that's true. If anything, she's impressed.

"Good idea," she says. "I have to leave here myself to go

meet with our insurance company. If we're getting any policy changes, I could probably use your help with them. But… we can sort all that out over email."

"Sure. I say. Sounds fine."

She leaves. And so that's it. I can leave, too.

Wow. That was easy. I'm free now. I can go wherever I want.

Good. Do it, then. Go ahead. Leave.

Okay, I will. I really will.

Except… I need closure somehow. It will feel too weird without *some* kind of closure. On a normal day, the clock reaching 5:00 gives me that closure. Walking out with Jannelle and the twins gives me closure.

So… what, then? I need a sign. A signal.

A bell, maybe? I have a little decorative bell on my desk. I got it from the craft table at the county fair a few years ago. It's white with black spots like a cow - making it, yes, a mini cowbell. I could use that to end my day. But no, a bell ringing would be too much like high school.

How about a whistle? You know, one of those train whistle things that they use to signal the end of work? Yes. Good idea.

I search the web for an audio clip. Turns out it's called a factory whistle. I press play and it makes the 'toot' sound twice. Perfect.

I pack up all my stuff, and I stand up to leave. And yes, I feel exposed somehow, all of the sudden. But anything worth doing is worth doing with confidence, right? That's a phrase I made up a long time ago. I mean, I pretty much never follow it, if you haven't noticed. But I still believe it's true, and there's no time like the present. So I try it now.

I pick up my three bags and I walk down the long middle aisle between the cubicles. Some people do look up at me as I pass, but probably only because I'm staring at them so self-consciously. Still, here I am. I'm doing it. I'm walking down this aisle. Alone. Just me and these overstuffed bags.

I'm coming, Wanda. I'm coming, Nelly. I'm coming,

Powder.

And I'm just about to get to the end and take a right towards the elevator that will bring to freedom, when up pops... wait for it... Aaron.

Of all people.

"Eliza," he says, looking at my bags, and then checking his watch. "Is everything okay?"

"Oh, sure. Everything is fine," I say, brushing off the question. "I just decided to knock off a little early today. Finish the rest at home."

The trouble is, even though Aaron and I aren't together anymore, we still know each other. As in, *know* each other. And he immediately senses that something's on my mind. That's the thing about exes: you can break off the relationship, but you can't break off knowing each other.

"*You* decided to knock off early?" he says. "You weren't sent home or something."

"No," I say. "Not at all."

And I want to end this conversation so bad that I'm ready to just start running out of here. But - *are you kidding me?* - to make the situation even more awkward, Ashley is heading our way, blocking my escape path. She's coming up from the elevators, staring at a document in her hand as she walks, so that she doesn't notice us until she's right here. That makes her look up all the sudden, startled, and I feel like I've been caught in the act of having a 'moment' with Aaron - her current boyfriend and my once-and-former boyfriend.

I mean, obviously this 'moment' is awkward, and it's short - as in 'already over and done with,' I sincerely hope. And it doesn't mean anything. Aaron's not flirting with me. If anything, he's playing this 'older brother' role he's developed since we broke up, where he does things like make sure I'm okay all the time.

Despite all that, it still doesn't feel right for her.

And you know what? I actually feel bad for her, because I give Ashley credit for one thing: when she got together with

Aaron, she made sure that I knew that there'd been nothing between them while he and I were still dating. Not even flirting. She said she'd never want to interfere in someone else's relationship.

And call me naive, but I believed her when she told me that.

The problem towards the end of my relationship with Aaron wasn't her. She's always treated me well. The only thing I've ever had against her, if anything, is that she just happened to be Aaron's next girlfriend.

So now that Aaron and I aren't together anymore, I'd like to treat her well, too.

"Hi Ashley," I say. "That's a nice dress."

She pauses for two mildly suspicious seconds, and then she says, "Thanks."

"You're welcome," I say. "I was just telling Aaron here that I'm leaving to go work from home. I know you two are going out on a sales call together. Good luck with it. I hope you have a good afternoon."

I'm well aware that I don't sound relaxed or natural as I say this, but the feeling is still there. And fortunately it does seem to come across, because after she pauses for a few more slightly less-suspicious seconds, she says, "Same to you."

And I walk out, exhausted from this ninety second social interaction that felt like it took six years. Maybe this is why I never leave early. It's just too complicated.

And as I wait for the elevator (hurry up, please), I can just *feel* that Aaron is still watching me with this newly minted 'brotherly concern' thing that makes me want to just bust out of here.

So… whatever, Aaron. Whatever for you.

Wanda and Nelly are the ones I want to focus on when I finally, *finally*, get out of the office and down to my car.

Here I come.

Box Streets, part II

I drive out of Office Park World, back to Teabridge. The freeway traffic jam is gone, and my car races and flows as I cut across lanes, passing one car and then another - just like my thoughts race and flow as I picture the rest of the afternoon. By the time I reach my exit off the interstate, my mind is finally sorted: I'll start by going to Wanda's house again, just to see if anything new is going on there, and that will give me the excuse I need to text Nelly.

I drive down Route 5 until I turn into Wanda's neighborhood on the left.

This morning, the area looked like just a bunch of confusingly indistinguishable square streets. But now on this second visit of the day, I have a sense of the place. I 'get' it now. We studied a little about this area in a local history unit in high school, actually, and everything I learned back then falls into place.

The grid pattern of these streets was intentionally created as part of the New England textile boom of the 1800's: larger corner houses with full front porches for the management; small but cute houses in the middle of each block to attract the more highly-skilled laborers from Lowell.

Wanda's house isn't quite like either of those. It sits just one lot away from the corner, and it's got a distinctive, smart style to it: the dormers in the roof, a patterned frieze above the porch columns, and bay windows on the garden side. I'm thinking maybe the local doctor lived here back in the day. This house, like many of the others around here, is original to the period - making it well over a hundred years old. Yet it's so well cared for, with a fresh paint job, new gutters, and a repointed chimney. It feels like the house has every intention of being here, just as sweet as ever, for decades to come. Like Wanda herself, I sincerely hope.

A noise brings me out of my mental walk through history -

specifically, a meow.

Powder is sitting on the front porch. When she sees that I've finally noticed her, she stands up and paces, so I open the gate and walk up toward the house. As soon as I step onto the porch, she rubs against my leg.

I bend down to pet her, and she meows even louder. In short, she's hungry. And ready to go inside.

I ring the bell. I knock. I even try the handle.

I look through the window near the door. I can see inside better than I could this morning. Wanda's home is neat and tastefully decorated. No surprise there. A beautiful patchwork quilt hangs on the wall at the far end of the entry hallway - blues and greys, framed by the baby blue wall around it. An earth tone quilt covers the sofa in the living room.

It all looks very cozy. And even quieter than it was this morning, if that's possible.

I look over at the neighbor's house - the same neighbor who peeked through the window at me earlier. And... she's there. When I look right at that same window, the curtain falls closed. She's spying on me again. "The nerve of her," I think, painfully aware that I'm in the middle of my own spying mission.

But what's different from this morning is that this time, she doesn't retreat back into her house and disappear. Instead, she emerges from the front door and calls over to me.

"You didn't feed her this morning," she says. Cranky.

"You mean the cat?" I say.

"Yes, I mean the cat. You didn't feed her."

"No, I didn't," I say. "But..."

I walk toward her to close the gap - and hopefully lower the volume of the conversation.

"I had to do it," she says, interrupting. "I had to feed her."

"Um... I didn't know I was supposed to feed her."

"Aren't you here to take care of the cat?"

"No. I'm just a friend of hers," I say. "I mean, kind of a friend. I know her from her shop downtown. But I haven't seen her in a few days, and I was just a little concerned about her. Has she been around?"

She looks at me for a few seconds - deciding whether to trust me, I suppose. Apparently I pass the test, because she responds to my question. "Not since Tuesday."

"You haven't seen Wanda at all since..."

"I felt bad for the cat, so fed her yesterday," she interrupts, again. "But you can't feed stray cats, because once they know you're soft, they'll never leave you alone."

I can't picture any creature, human or animal, ever thinking this woman is soft. But despite her suspicious nature and stern old New England tone, she *is* looking out for Wanda. Or Powder, at least.

"I'd like to help the cat, but I don't have a key." I say. "I can't let her in to feed her or anything."

"Then you better take her with you," she says. "She'll freeze out here."

Okay, there's a lot wrong with those statements. For one thing, Powder is not going to freeze out here because she's as furry as a bag of wool. And it's not even cold outside right now. Plus - I mean, *really* - I can't steal Wanda's cat from her front porch. I just can't. And that's what I'd basically be doing if I took her out of here: stealing her.

I mean... Wanda would forgive me for doing it if she found out. She'd be glad, even, that someone she knows was taking care of her cat.

And Powder seems to like me, which is good news. She hasn't stopped rubbing back and forth against my ankle, purring away like a ceiling fan the whole time I've been standing here.

But still.

I can't.

Powder probably wouldn't even let me pick her up to bring her to the car. I mean, I know she's giving me plenty of affection, but cats like to do things on their own terms - not yours.

So… wait. Okay, now I've picked her up, and she's totally letting me. She even seems to like it. She settles into the crook of my arm, purring even louder.

But there's no way she'd let me put her into my car. Every cat I've ever met hates cars. I can already hear the deep, unhappy meows she's going to make when I…

Okay. She's in the car. And she's fine.

I mean, she does meow. She meows plenty. But these are more curious meows than angry or plaintive. Just wondering where we're headed, I suppose.

I drive out of Wanda's neighborhood, still watched by the neighbor across the street. She's back at her window, and she nods as I drive away, which is the closest thing I'll get to a goodbye from her. That's okay. I'll take it.

As I pull into downtown Teabridge. I'm warmed by all the familiar sights - the stores, the people, the street itself. This is my home. The place I love. The people I love.

I park in the lot behind Bank Row.

The debris that Griff and his boys left strewn around the dumpster is still here, though now it's kicked into a single pile. There's a note taped to the top. It says,

Refuse must be placed inside the dumpster. Building scraps are not allowed.

The building supervisor must have seen the mess, and he wrote the note to scold the perpetrator. Good. Take that, Griff.

I leave my bags in the car along with (I can't believe I'm saying this) the *cat,* and I walk to the end of the alley that opens onto the street. Devin's in front of the dollar store. He's banging something. Loud, as usual.

He's got his noise-reducing safety earphones on, so he's in his own world. I take a wide berth around his ladder, out into the street. He's focused on his work and doesn't notice me.

Except when I curve back in, towards the door of Wanda's

shop, he gives me a sidelong glance. A quick flash that says yes, he knows I'm here. And he's known it since I stepped out of the alley.

I nod to him. It's subtle, but he notices.

There are no customers inside Wanda's shop at the moment, though I see signs of today's busyness. The dish bucket is full. The newspaper is strewn about in sections on the coffee table, on the seat of the easy chair, and on one of the cafe tables. The display cases are nearly empty of baked goods. What I can see of the kitchen has flour and dough and ingredients strewn about. It's like a giant muffin exploded back there.

And the door to the back hallway is open. Nelly is in there, standing stone-still as she looks out the window in the rear door. Her weight is on one foot while the other is poised in the middle of lifting - frozen, mid-step, by some noise. A voice, or a danger of some kind.

"Nelly?" I call to her. And I guess I underestimated how well sound carries in this place, because she whirls around, startled.

"You!" she says.

She rushes toward me.

What? Is she angry or something?

"Oh my gosh, I am *so* glad to see you!" she says.

I guess she's not angry.

She stops short, just a foot away. She was about to hug me but then thought better of it, out of politeness. After all, we met only this morning. But though we're not quite at the 'hug-hello' stage of friendship yet, she certainly looks like she could use a hug, so I put a hand on her shoulder, at least.

I'm just about to ask her if she's okay, but her eyes suddenly dart around the main room.

"Oh - no customers?" she says. "Finally!"

She scoots over to the front door, spins the Open sign to Closed, and locks the handle.

"Don't get me wrong," she says. "Wanda's customers are

great, but this has been quite a day. I went through a full sack of flour making muffins, which are all gone, by the way. And the whole time, I'm trying to keep an eye on the discount store boys. And is it just me, or are they totally up to something? I mean, I don't know. I need your perspective. I'm way too close to this right now."

This morning, she doubted my whole 'Wanda's gone missing' story. If anything, she was amused by the whole thing, like it was some fun caper.

But she's in full crisis mode now.

"What were you just looking at out back?" I ask her. "Was it them? Are they out there?"

"No," she says. "I don't know. I keep… hearing things. Do you hear things?"

"What things?"

"Well, first of all, there's so much construction noise from your boyfriend."

"My *boyfriend?*"

"Yeah, Devin."

"Devin is *not* my -"

"Okay. Fine," she says. "That's not my point. My point is there's so much noise from him and from the discount store guys - coming and going, moving boxes. Their store doesn't seem to be any more of a store than it was yesterday, but for some reason they're still always making noise. And then every once in a while, things get quiet, and I…"

She cuts herself off in mid-sentence, wincing.

"What?" I say. "You have to tell me. Isn't that your rule from this morning? If you start to say something, you have to finish it?"

"Alright, alright," she says. She takes a breath. "Fine. I'll say it: I think I hear Wanda."

"You mean, you really miss Wanda, and every once in a while when you have a memory of her, you hear her voice in your head? Is that what you mean? Or do you mean…"

"I think I actually hear her," Nelly says. "I mean, you tell me. Devin has stopped nailing, which means his compressor will turn off any moment now. So let's just… wait…"

We wait. And she's right: when Devin is fully engaged, he makes so much noise, but when the compressor does turn off a few seconds later, it's a different world all the sudden.

And then…

I hear a voice. That is, I think I do. Coming from, I don't know, the walls or something. Or just… the air.

But it's hard to tell for sure. I mean, we're on a main street. It's an extremely quiet main street, I know - but still, people pass by, and they talk. And they call to each other. So it's hard to really know for sure what we're hearing.

Plus now there's all this new banging out back. The discount boys are slamming their rear door, breaking up boxes, opening the dumpster lid and then letting it drop back down. Everything they do makes a racket, and it erases not just the sound we heard - if we actually did hear something - but it erases my whole train of thought as well.

Nelly, on the other hand, has had more practice with all this commotion, because she's onto something. She's walking, slowly but deliberately, towards the door to the basement. She looks at me with a 'Come on!' look on her face.

"What are you doing?" I say, as I join her.

"I heard something downstairs," she says. "I think I did, anyway."

"What's down there?" I ask her.

"I don't know. Baking supplies, I hope. Because I really am out of flour."

"You mean you haven't gone down there yet?"

"No," she says. "If you remember, we called down this morning to see if Wanda was there. But when we didn't hear anything, I didn't bother with it. And I've been completely busy ever since then."

"Okay, well," I say. "We should probably check."

I turn on my cell phone flashlight until we find a switch on the wall.

We walk down. Nelly is in front, but we're so crowded together we're practically on top of each other. Then I realize that these old wooden stairs creak really loud when we step on one at the same time, so I drop back and follow.

The hallway at the bottom takes a quick, sharp, left turn and then curves around itself into a right turn through an open door. Sort of. I mean, it's kind of confusing. We step through into the next hallway, and we walk. Along the sides there's a dusty old broom and a dented metal dust pan.

The end of the hallway opens up into a cramped storage room full of office equipment: broken shelves, a rusty metal filing cabinet, and an old office chair with cushions eaten away by mice. One wall has a bunch of what looks like easels - not like an artist would use, but more like what you'd see at a business meeting to hold the graphs and charts. The other walls are bare, except for a single door that's boarded up with a plank.

I look at Nelly. She looks back at me. She's obviously noticed there are no baking supplies down here at all. No sacks of flour. No pots and pans. No deep freezer. Just dust and old office furniture.

"Now I'm really going crazy," Nelly says. "I swear I remember coming down here to get supplies at least once when I worked here two summers ago, but now I'm questioning everything."

Just to check, she opens one of the drawers of the filing cabinet, which collapses into a clanging mess.

And then there's total silence.

No noise from Devin's power equipment. No clanging of the dumpster from the discount store guys.

And in this silence, we hear a thumping. It's barely noticeable, but it's there.

And suddenly we feel like we're not alone down here.

Except... we really *are* alone down here. We have to be, because there's no place for anyone to be hiding. No place that we can see, anyway.

Nelly looks at me. "Do you think the discount boys heard the noise we just made?" she says.

"I hope not," I say. "Let's get out of here."

"Done."

We walk back down through the maze of hallways - which again totally do not go in the direction I thought they'd go. But we make it back to the stairs. And this time, we don't care how many creaking noises we make as we scurry up, back into the main room of the muffin shop.

We even go up near the sitting area, to be further away from the basement door, and then we grab each other's hands, sharing our fear.

"Let's go to my apartment," I say. "Do you...?"

"Yes!" she says, before I can even finish asking.

I unlock the door, and I'm about to go through it. But then I stop.

"What?" she says.

"I just remembered I left my work-bags in my car. And..."

"And what?"

"My bags are not the only thing in the car. Powder is in there too."

"Powder as in..."

"Wanda's cat," I say.

Nelly's eyes get extremely big.

"I'll explain when we get to my apartment," I say. "But in the meantime..."

"We have to go back to the parking lot," she says. "Somehow."

"That's no big deal, right? We'll just go out the front and curve around the alley, which won't be suspicious because they already know you're here, and they probably already know I park my car back there."

"Okay, maybe I'm just more freaked out than you are because I've been around these guys all day," Nelly says, "but I want to be more cautious than that."

At this moment, Devin's generator kicks on, reminding me

that he's out front. "Ooh - Devin could be our lookout," I tell her.

"Why would we ask him for help?" she says. "I know I teased you about him being your boyfriend. But, seriously, he works for them. He's *one of them*."

"No, I don't think he *is* 'one of them,'" I say. "He's an independent contractor, not an employee, and he's just as suspicious of them as we are. I trust him."

"So is he your boyfriend, or isn't he?"

"No! He's not! I knew him, a *little*, when I was in high school," I say. "That's all. And right now, you and I have to get out of here somehow, so can we just find out if he'll help us?"

"Fine," she says.

I step outside to the recessed entryway, and right away I'm hit with the noise of Devin's loud hydraulic nailer connected to the louder compressor and the even louder generator in the back of his van. Devin is nailing trim. And isn't this the same pointless task he was working on yesterday?

"Hey," I call to him, in a stage whisper. "Devin!"

His equipment is so loud that I figure there's no way he heard me, but he does stop working long enough for the compressor and generator to turn off.

So I call to him again. "Devin!"

He's staring straight at the piece of trim, and he doesn't bat an eye. He just slips one side of his protective headphones off his right ear and says, "I *see* you."

Hm. So he was obviously looking out for us already, just like he was looking out for me yesterday when I was in the discount store.

"Are they in there?" I ask.

He casually takes a few steps down the ladder, and then he glances into the storefront.

"Not now," he says. "But they're around somewhere. In the back room, I think."

"We need to get around to the parking lot, through the

alley."

"Both of you?"

"Yeah. Why? You don't think that's safe?" I say.

"The guys have been moving around all day," he says. "They could be anywhere at any moment. I don't want them to see you together."

"We'll go one at a time," I say, and I move aside so Nelly can go first.

She gets into the ready position, and I look up to Devin. "She's going under," I tell him.

"What?" he says.

And I think he's questioning the wisdom of it, so I come back with, "Don't worry, she's really fast. She was a sprinter in high school."

But he wasn't questioning my wisdom; he just didn't hear me. So he starts to come down off the ladder at the exact same time that Nelly emerges from her crouch, and they almost collide, sending Devin off the side of the ladder. I grab his arm to steady him, but - ahh! - now the ladder spins and rattles and falls toward me, looking very huge as it's about to crash down on my head.

So Devin drops his nailer - bang! - and he grabs the ladder just as I grab it too. We hold it for a moment, somehow, at an angle that the word 'skewed' does not begin to describe.

And why do we hold the ladder 'for a moment,' instead of immediately setting it back upright? Because in the commotion, he's turned his body toward me. And I've twisted my body to turn toward him.

And in this 'moment,' we have, well, a *moment*.

I'm looking right into his eyes. And he's looking right into mine.

And... what?

Feelings?

No.

What? No. Not at this crazy moment, surely. Stop this! Now! Someone, please help us stop this now!

"Guys," Nelly calls out (thank you, Nelly). "Guys!"

I shift the weight of the ladder to Devin, and he stands it back up. And we both wipe the puppy-dog looks off our faces.

And then I realize I'm pretty much in front of the discount store by this point - enough that I might as well just go all the way across. And do the discount boys see me clumsily rushing past their window? Are they in there? I don't know.

But what I do know for sure is that the three of us are the worst sneak-around-ers in the history of sneaking around.

And that doesn't even compare to what happens when Nelly and I get to the back parking lot. We grab everything from my car and stumble back through the alley and across the street, tripping over each other as we flail along with my way-too-many work bags under our arms - along with a very confused, very loud cat.

Nelly and I make a sloppy effort to disguise the fact of where my apartment is - despite how careful I've been up to this point. But at this moment, it's all we can do to stay upright.

Lace Curtain

When we finally get into my apartment, we dump my work bags on the floor, and then Powder leaps out of my arms and runs behind the couch.

Nelly and I stop and catch our breath a little.

"Well," I say. "That was quite an adventure."

"Mis-adventure is more like it," she says. "But we made it."

"Yes, look at us. We made it."

And Nelly does look down at her clothes, which are covered with flour and muffin batter and blueberry stains and… basically, she's covered with the muffin shop.

"Do you want to get cleaned up?" I say.

"That's probably a good idea."

I hand her a towel, and she goes to take a shower. While she's in there, I pick out something for her to change into. I could lend her some of my old clothes, but just as a nice gesture, I put out the flannel shirt I bought from the discount store yesterday, so that she'll have at least one nice, new thing to wear.

Then I sink down into my easy chair. I go on my laptop to review this afternoon's work emails and sort through a couple of tasks - just to get all this done so that when Nelly comes out of the shower, we can settle into the real matter at hand: Wanda.

While I'm working, I notice Powder eventually emerges from behind the couch and walks around, touching her nose to things. And if you think she doesn't notice SuperFuzz balled up on the couch, then you don't know cats. They have a sixth sense for cozy sleeping places.

I eye her as if to say, *Back off, kitty - that's _my_ SuperFuzz.*

And she eyes me right back: *Oh really? We'll just see about that, won't we?*

And here I am having a full-on imaginary conversation with a ten-pound animal.

Fi always teases me that I'm three cats away from being a crazy cat lady. Well, Fi - as of this moment, I'm two cats away.

Powder wins our face-off, by the way. Of course. Within a minute, she's tucked herself inside my blanket, purring contentedly. Or is she just gloating?

Nelly comes out wearing the discount store flannel shirt, along with the same jeans she had on at the shop.

"Why don't you sit down," I say, when I see how fast she's still breathing.

"Yeah," she says. "I think I'd better."

But she doesn't sit. Instead, she just paces in the only place in my apartment you *can* pace: between the coffee table and the back of the easy chair.

"Come," I say. I gesture toward the couch. She sits.

"Um…" she says. "It itches."

"What itches?"

"The shirt."

Ugh. Of course it itches. It's from the discount store.

And to add to that, her jeans somehow have just as much flour and batter on them as her shirt and apron did - even though the apron was full-length. Which, no, I have no idea how that could happen.

"I hate to ask," she says. "But can I do what you did?"

"What did I do?" I say.

"You put on pajamas."

"Huh?" I say. I look down at my clothes and… I'm wearing pajamas?

When did I put on pajamas? I don't know. I have no memory of doing it, so it must have happened while she was showering. Has getting into pajamas become such an automatic thing for me at this point that I don't even notice it's happening?

Well. Anyway. At least I won't be alone. I get Nelly my lime green pair with orange polka dots. They make her look like a cartoon leopard - but a very comfortable one.

We settle in.

"Okay, so let's just sort through this," I say. "And you can start by telling me what happened today. Because when we last talked this morning, you doubted anything was wrong at all."

"Well that's the thing: it's hard to know," she says. "But all day, whenever I'd do anything out back, like bring an empty box to the dumpster or something, they'd be there. And they'd stop whatever they were doing and look at me sideways. And I could never figure out what, exactly, they were doing, except that it involved boxes and tools and a lot of noise and sneaking around. And the whole thing has put me in this weird place where on the one hand I want to call the police. But on the other hand, I still keep hoping Aunt Wanda's going to call at any moment and say, 'Thanks for taking over the shop while I'm on vacation. I'm having a great time.'"

"Right," I say. "And to be absolutely clear, you didn't get any call from her at all - not a voicemail or anything?"

"Well... can I show you something?"

"Yes, please," I say.

She takes out her phone. "I didn't tell you about this earlier this morning, because I was afraid you'd laugh at me for being too weird," she says. "You won't laugh, will you?"

"How could I, at this point?"

"Okay," she says. "You know I got that first email from her on Tuesday saying, 'Sure, come visit me - I'd love to have you'? Well, for the next day or so, I didn't hear from her at all. But I didn't make a big deal of it, because like I said earlier, we've done this whole thing before where I schedule a visit at the last minute. But then, finally, early this morning - like, really early, before I even left the hotel I stayed at in New Jersey on my way here - I did get an email from her. That's what I didn't tell you before, because it was just too weird."

"What was so weird about the email?" I say.

"It's a recipe for lemon-curd loaf."

"That doesn't sound weird," I say. "In fact, it sounds pretty good."

"Does it, though?" she says. "I don't think you'll feel that way when you see this..."

She shows me the recipe on her phone, nodding solemnly. "You get it, right?"

"Um, I get that it's a recipe for lemon curd loaf. But...?"

"Look closely. It says, 'Add a half-cup of lemon juice to a half-cup of milk, and beat until smooth.'"

"Okay," I say. "So?"

"Straight, fresh lemon juice would totally curdle the milk," she says.

"But it's lemon-*curd* loaf."

"You make lemon curd with lemon, sugar, eggs, and butter - not with milk."

"What do you make with lemon and milk?"

"A mess," she says. "The recipe is wrong. It has to be."

"So she made a mistake."

"A deliberate mistake," she says. "She's sending us a message."

"Not a very clear one," I say. "Why wouldn't she just come out and say what she has to say?"

"I don't know," Nelly says - but clearly she *does* know, or thinks she does, because she's looking at me, eagerly.

"Alright, out with it," I say.

She leans toward me, so she can talk lower. "I'm just thinking... What if Wanda's been, like, kidnapped or something, and they're letting her communicate with us in these apparently harmless emails, just to give us the impression that everything is okay?"

"You're saying they're monitoring the emails, so she's sending us secret messages..."

"By hiding them in the form of bad recipes!" Nelly says. "I'm now convinced the discount boys have something to do with Wanda's disappearance."

"Wow, that's really weird."

"What? You don't agree with me?"

"Actually, just the opposite," I say. "These are all things I've thought about myself. What's weird is having someone else say them. I feel like I should take on my sister's role of the doubter, just to keep the balance. Fi's always been the steady one. The realist."

"Well, it's fine with me if you want to bring some sanity to the room," Nelly says.

"I'll try," I say. "So, to be triple-clear, the only contact you've gotten from Wanda since Tuesday is the weird-recipe email?"

"The only 'anything' I've gotten from her is the weird recipe," Nelly says. "And yes, I checked every folder in my regular email and my school email: Spam. Trash. Deleted texts. Wanda's social media for her business. Everything."

"And you were at the muffin shop all day," I say.

"All day," she says. "From the time you left for work to the time you got back home."

"And were the discount store guys around all that time?"

"The whole time."

"What were they doing?"

"Like I said, moving boxes. Moving around. Making noise. They keep busy - that's for sure."

"So they should have made a lot of progress on the store, then," I say. "Have they?"

"Not that I can tell," she says. "But I've never been inside it."

"I have," I say. "And I remember it in vivid detail, because it was one of those scary moments that makes you notice everything. So you know what? Devin is still outside in front of their store. Let's text him and ask him to take a picture of the inside."

"Do you know his number?"

"It's not hard to find," I say.

I look out through the lace curtains at his van parked in the street, with the side labeled in those big, bold, airbrushed letters: *Devin Wahl Does it All - 555-3812.*

I send him a text: *Devin - it's Lizzie from across the street. And, you know, high school.*

I see him pause on his ladder. He takes out his phone, and in a moment, I get his reply: *Hi Lizzie from high school. R u ok?*

I write back: *Fine. But... favor: take a picture of the inside of the store?*

He reads my message and casually pretends to type out a long response, while subtly moving his phone right up to the window. Within a minute, he sends me three photos.

"Look, Nelly. The showroom of the store hasn't changed one bit in the last twenty-four hours," I say, showing her my phone. "I don't know what they're doing over there, but they're not building a store."

"So let's do it," she says. "Let's call the police."

"I'd like to," I say. "But what are we going to tell them?"

"I don't know - that those guys have been acting suspicious?"

"Suspicious is a relative term," I say. "Dirty looks from creepy guys isn't documentable evidence."

"Well, it should be."

"I agree," I say. "But I'm just telling you what Fi tells me. And for better or worse, she would know."

"So how do we handle this?"

"I have an idea," I say.

I look up the non-emergency line at the police station, and I show it to Nelly. "Use this number," I say. "And just be casual. Give them the 'it's probably nothing' routine. That way, if they send someone over to check all this out, it will be their idea, not ours."

She nods and dials the number on her phone, tilting the earpiece in my direction. I lean in close. A man answers. "Teabridge police. Is this an emergency?"

"No, it's not an emergency," Nelly says. "At least I hope it isn't."

I can hear the urgency in Nelly's voice because I know her,

but she does a pretty good job of keeping it in check for the officer.

"What seems to be the problem?" the man says.

"I haven't heard from my aunt Wanda in a few days. She owns the muffin shop in town. Do you know it?"

"Cottage Street?" he says.

"That's the place," Nelly says. "I just moved back to town, and she was supposed to meet me at the shop this morning. But she hasn't been around all day."

"And that's unusual?"

"She's pretty reliable," Nelly says.

"Uh-huh," the man says. Then he's quiet for a moment.

This feels like a moment of truth. Nelly looks at me and whispers, "Should I say something more? Give details? I don't want him to just shrug us off."

I shake my head: No, just wait.

Nelly cringes: she doesn't want to wait.

Then we catch a break. "Hold on," the officer says. "I'll see if anyone's available."

We get put on hold, which is fine with me. Time to breathe.

I nod to Nelly. This is now going as I'd hoped. The police are the ones deciding how seriously to take this; we just called the non-emergency line, that's all.

A woman clicks into the line. "Officer Julia Ramos. How can I help you?"

I smile. This is the same woman Fi is friends with, and I know she's a good person to deal with.

"Just trying to track down my aunt," Nelly says. "She didn't show up for work today, and I'm a little concerned."

"Okay, tell me what you know."

Nelly gives the details. I gently squeeze her arm each time she gets too excited or says too much - which she seems to like because it helps her stay even-keeled.

Then, an interesting question from Officer Ramos: "Who was the last person to speak to your aunt?"

Nelly squints. It wasn't her, because she hasn't actually spoken to Wanda in a few weeks. Instead, they've done all their recent correspondence through emails and texts.

So was it me on Tuesday morning? I don't think so, because there were still customers in the shop when I left for work that day.

I take a deep breath. And then I point to the discount store. Them.

Nelly's eyes light up again. She likes the idea. A lot.

"I believe that a neighboring business owner was the last one to talk to Wanda," she says to Officer Ramos.

"Have you spoken to them?"

"No," Nelly says. "They're brand new, and I don't even know them yet, so I just thought it would be easier if…"

"That's fine," Officer Ramos says. "I'll do it. See if we can get this sorted out for you. What's your name?"

"Nelly Beecher," she says. And then she adds - I don't know why - "And Lizzie Groff."

"Groff, you say?"

Ugh. Fi uses her full name at work, including her maiden name - which is, yes, the same last name as mine: Groff. And Officer Ramos clearly recognizes it.

Now my eyes light up. I whisper, too loud, "Why did you tell her my name?"

"I don't want to do this alone," Nelly whispers back, even louder.

Oh, well. What's done is done.

"Give me an hour," Officer Ramos says.

"Should we meet you somewhere?" Nelly says.

"Let me check it out first, and I'll call you later. Is this a number where you can be reached?"

"Yes. I'll leave my phone on," Nelly says. "And thank you."

So there it is. We've taken a big step. And now there's nothing to do but wait.

I go back to the window. I don't sit in the easy chair because I'm just too worked up for that. And you know you're in a bad state when you don't want to sit in an easy chair. I mean, it's *called* an easy chair. Why *wouldn't* you want to sit in it?

But I can't. Not now.

I force myself to sit at my desk and finish my last remaining TechTile work for today, while Nelly takes a turn by the window. She's really just as worked up as I am, but she stays put by busying herself with the binoculars, then her phone, then the binoculars, then… well, you get the idea.

From my desk, I can still hear the cars pass by slow and easy, like ocean waves.

Occasionally I hear one stop and idle. Each time it happens, I look up at Nelly, but each time she tells me it's just someone who's stopped to let a pedestrian pass by, or to drop someone off at the bank - which happens more than I would have thought. It's interesting what you notice when you really pay attention.

I finish up my work for the day. Then, the fun part: I take out my calligraphy pen and make tomorrow's to-do list. And boy, I really like doing this - carefully writing each letter with all the extra curls and swirls. I want to show my list to Nelly because I think she'd get a kick out of it. But when I look up at her, I see her staring off into the distance, reflectively. And only now do I realize how quiet she's been for several minutes, actually. It's quite a change from the excitement and distraction of all our sneaking around and spying. And in this quiet moment of reflection, the reality of the whole situation is hitting her hard.

"I'm sorry for all this," I say. "I know how much Wanda means to me, and I'm just a customer. I can barely imagine what she must mean to you."

"Yeah," Nelly says. "But whatever. She's just my aunt, though."

She forces her voice to sound casual as she minimizes her

feelings toward her aunt, but emotions this deep are hard to hide. Fi's psychology books call it 'reaction formation': when an emotion is too hard to face, you act like the opposite is true.

"Right," I say. "Except she took care of you when you were younger."

She takes a long pause. "Well, my Dad had to drive my Mom back and forth to Boston for special treatments. They didn't want a little kid tagging along, so they sent me to Wanda's just to get me out of the way."

"You said that earlier, and I felt bad for you," I say. "But I thought about it some more, and what if they weren't just trying to get you out of the way?"

I'm pushing a little, I know. But it feels right in the moment. I mean, I think about this kind of thing all the time, so maybe I should try actually saying it more often. And Nelly is such a nice person; she deserves some encouragement. So I continue. "Did you ever think that maybe they sent you to Wanda's because they wanted what was best for you, too? It's not my business, I know, but maybe they weren't just getting rid of you. Maybe they were trying to give you a good home life with Wanda because they had to focus so much on your Mom."

Nelly starts to say something. But all she gets out is, "Yeah?"

"I mean, I don't know for sure, obviously, because I wasn't there," I say. "But what do you think? Could that be true?"

She closes her eyes for a moment. Then she opens them and looks right at me. "I don't know why, but I never thought of it that way before," she says. "You're right about one thing, for sure: Wanda gave me a good home during the hardest period of my life. That's the real reason I keep coming back here, to tell you the truth: so I can spend more time with her. I shouldn't have talked about her in such an off-handed way a few minutes ago, and I'm sorry I did that."

I put my hand on her shoulder and smile as if to say, *It's okay. It's nothing.*

"I don't know what's wrong with me. Maybe I'm just hungry."

"Hungry. Yes. Not a bad theory," I say. "You've been sustaining yourself for twelve hours on muffin crumbs and coffee. A real dinner will do you good."

For better or worse, my version of a real dinner is two microwavable diet meals - trays with separate compartments for chicken with lemon sauce, three broccoli florets, and some mashed squash. And no, I'm not on a diet; I just like to eat my dinner out of little compartments.

Plus, of course, less time cooking means more time staring out the window. I slide one of the dining room chairs next to Nelly, and I manage to actually sit down this time. We both lean forward and look through the curtain while we eat our tray-dinners and wait for the police to show up, like the whole world of Teabridge is a movie that we're watching.

Halfway through our meal, it happens: a cruiser rolls up in front of the muffin shop. Officer Ramos, no doubt. She gets out casually. She's around my age, maybe a little older. Perfect. I'm thinking she's experienced enough to handle this whole thing calmly, while still being young enough to forgive the possible overreactions of two crazy girls with big imaginations.

Ramos goes up to Wanda's shop and looks inside. She tries the door. Locked. A man walks by on the street and stops next to her. I recognize him as one of the bank tellers, and I know he goes into Wanda's most mornings for coffee on his way into work. He and Ramos talk for a minute, but he ends the conversation by shaking his head. So he knows nothing either, unfortunately.

Now Ramos turns to Devin, who's at the back of his van, sorting his tools - though I'm pretty sure he's just pretending to sort his tools while he eavesdrops on Ramos. She walks up to him and they chat. He nods and leans towards her as they speak, encouraging her to ask more questions and get more involved.

Then all the sudden because - this is interesting - Griff and Cory walk out the front door of the discount store. They're right in the middle of an argument, as usual - caught up in their own issues.

But when they do see Ramos, Griff does more than stop short: he freezes like a deer. After a moment - too long, really - he forces a smile on his face and greets her. They chat for a moment. Griff shakes his head 'no' at nearly every one of her questions - in an exaggerated way, overselling the 'I know nothing' routine that Ramos clearly isn't buying for a second.

Cory seethes this whole time, seeing all too clearly how much Griff is in over his head. If you ask me, Cory should find a new gang, because he's way too sharp for Griff. He could do well for himself if he found some partners-in-crime who didn't frustrate him so much. Actually, he should find a different line of work entirely: an honest one.

Ramos finishes her line of questioning. Then she points to Devin's van and says a few more things before handing Griff her business card. Griff nods even more ingratiatingly, but does he really think Ramos is buying this? When she finally dismisses him, he and Cory walk back into the discount store - though 'flee' is a better word to describe the way Griff moves.

When they're completely gone, Ramos walks over to her cruiser, leans against it, and makes a call.

Nelly's phone rings.

"Officer Ramos!" Nelly says, as soon as she picks up.

Ramos, amused by Nelly's immediate, enthusiastic greeting, looks around like she's expecting us to pop out of a manhole cover or something.

"Miss Beecher," Ramos says. "Where are you…?"

"Up in an apartment across the street," Nelly says.

Ramos glances up at our window, and even from this distance, I swear I can see her rolling her eyes.

"Listen, I made a few calls back in the office," she continues. "Spoke to a few of your Aunt's relatives. No one seemed to know much. They weren't too concerned either, to tell you the truth. And I just spoke to the owners of the shop next to Wanda's. They say they saw her a few days ago. Couldn't say exactly when because they've been so busy getting their place up and running."

"And you believed them?" Nelly says. "Because we don't. We think they've taken Wanda."

"They seem a bit shifty to be opening a retail store, I'll give you that," Ramos says. "But at this point, I have no reason to actually suspect them of anything. They answered my questions and told me they saw your aunt Wanda on Tuesday, and she mentioned going away for a few days. They said they'd let me know if she showed up again. I ended by telling them to get this carpenter's van off the street by the end of the week, and he promised it would be gone by five o'clock on Friday."

"So that's it?"

"In the absence of something more to go on, yes."

Nelly sighs in response, and Ramos picks up on it right away. "I understand if you're worried about your aunt," she says. "But until we learn otherwise, what we're dealing with here is simply a woman who's gone on vacation. I assume you haven't heard anything new in the last hour?"

"No," Nelly says, deflated. "Nothing new."

"Alright, well I plan to swing by your aunt's house, though from what you told me earlier, there's not much to see there. I'll circulate her photo among the departments in the area, and they'll keep an eye out. And I'll just ask you to continue to do the same. Let me know if anything turns up, or if you remember anything that could be useful."

"Yes, I will," Nelly says, as they end their call. "Of course. And thank you."

She means the 'thank you' part, but she can't hide how disappointed she is. We both are.

And my disappointment doubles as I see a dark blue sedan roll up and park right behind Ramos' cruiser. A very familiar dark blue sedan.

Fi. My sister.

She's driving her work-car, not the minivan that I'm used to seeing her in. But it's just as recognizable to me, especially when Fi herself gets out.

When Ramos recognized my last name during the earlier phone call with Nelly, she must have made a courtesy call to my sister - who then interrupted whatever she was doing to run over here.

I watch her and Ramos chat casually. Fi squints and smiles, probably apologizing for the trouble I'm causing. I mean, I don't think I'm the one causing the trouble; the discount store guys are the ones causing it. But I admit I haven't done enough to convince anyone else of that - besides Nelly, that is. And for that matter, Devin, too, who has managed to remain standing at the back of his van monitoring the whole situation, while somehow not making it obvious that he's been adjusting the same wrench for ten minutes now.

Fi and Ramos eventually part ways, and Fi waits until the cruiser has driven completely off before she crosses the street, heading right for my building.

I put down my dinner tray and rush out the door, down the stairs.

When I get to the bottom, Fi is standing in the foyer, looking at the names next to each buzzer, trying to figure out which one is mine. She's been here a million times, so it should be second nature to her by now. But one thing I know about Fi is that when non-work things - like, ugh, *me* - interrupt her actual work life, she gets frustrated. And when she's frustrated, she's distracted, especially about little things like apartment numbers. I don't want to risk her pressing the wrong buzzer and disturbing a neighbor, so I skip down the final six steps and open the door.

"Come in," I say quickly, like I've been expecting her the whole time. Which I have.

She comes in.

"Hurry," I say. "They could come back at any second."

"*Who* could come back?" she says.

"Just come on," I say.

We scuttle up the stairs. I scuttle, that is. Fi walks with the even, measured steps of a grade school principal bringing a misbehaving student to the detention room.

And when we get up to my apartment, she folds her arms and stares at me. So now she *looks* like a grade school principal, too.

"There I was, finishing up my work day," she says, "and I'm just about to leave to go home to dinner with my family when I get a call from Julia Ramos."

"Yeah, I can explain," I say.

But she interrupts me. "Lizzie," she says. And I know that her next words are going to be, 'Really, now.'

As in, 'Lizzie. *Really* now - how could you?'

So I interrupt her right back. "Fi, I know how it looks to you. But trust me, this whole thing with Wanda really is something."

"*Really* something," Nelly adds.

"And you are...?" Fi says, just now noticing we're not alone.

"Nelly Beecher," she says. "I'm Wanda's niece."

And I don't know if it's just politeness in front of a stranger, or if my sister is actually impressed that I have a corroborating witness to whatever nonsense I'm up to, but she straightens up, a bit more willing to hear what we have to say.

"Can we tell you our story?" I ask. "I know you're going to be super skeptical, but that's fine with me, because I tried to be the 'realistic one' earlier today, but you're better at it. And we'd much rather be wrong than right. So... will you help us?"

Fi checks her watch. "I've already missed dinner, so I might as well hear it."

"If you're hungry, I could zap you a Healthy Life," I say.

Fi slow-burns and says, "Lizzie, *really* now."

I guess she had to get that phrase in somehow.

"Alright, you go first," Nelly says, "since you were the first one to notice she was gone."

"Sure," I say, "That sounds g--"

"Plus I'll probably just interrupt you anyway when I have something to say."

I laugh. "Oh - so you do know that about yourself?"

She scrunches her face up, exaggerating embarrassment. "A little."

"Alright," I say. "Fi, it all started when I heard this noise on Tuesday morning - a banging or a clanging or something. And when I looked out my window, I saw Wanda out in front of her shop, looking in the direction of the discount store."

"Yes, you told me about this," Fi says. "But noises happen all the time around here. Teabridge may be small, but this is one of the main streets."

"But why did this noise bring Wanda out of her shop, when she's usually so immersed in baking at that hour?"

"Good question," Nelly says.

"Thank you," I say. "So I went to work on Tuesday, but I kept having this feeling…"

"A *feeling*," Fi says, sarcastically.

"Yes, Fi - a feeling. Like, were you ever playing hide-and-go-seek when you were a kid, and you go into a room to look for the hiders, and you just know - you can just *feel* - that someone's in there? Like, I don't know, maybe you can hear their breathing? Not enough to consciously hear it, but enough to *know* that someone's there. Is this making sense?"

"Oh, totally," Nelly says, jumping in to back me up. "It's like you don't know how you know, but you *know*."

"Exactly," I say. "And if nothing else had happened, I would have let it drop. But the feeling lingered, for sure. And Wednesday morning…"

"You mean yesterday?" Fi asks.

"Yes, yesterday - though it feels like a week ago. I go down for a muffin like usual. And the front door of Wanda's shop was really hard to open."

"Are you saying you broke in the front door?"

"No!" I say. "Not at all! I just… kept shaking the door until it opened. Does that sound like 'breaking in'?"

"Yes," Fi says. "It does."

"Well, whatever it is, I went inside, and I could tell Wanda hadn't been there at all that morning. And then the next thing I know, these three shady guys are opening this Dollar Discount in the empty storefront next to Wanda's. Nelly and I think they've taken Wanda."

"We're convinced of it," Nelly chimes in.

"And Devin thinks so, too," I say.

"Who?"

"The carpenter that was out by his truck just now when you were talking to Officer Ramos. Devin Wahl."

"Why do I know that name?"

"I knew him in high school a little. He's got his own business now, and he's doing a job for the discount store guys."

"Didn't you and he used to have a thing for each other?" Fi says.

Nelly nods.

"What? No!" I squeal. "Why does everyone keep saying that he and I… You know what? Forget it - it's not important. Listen, Fi, I've been watching this whole thing pretty much non-stop for, like, three days now, and I know something's going on. And… why is that suddenly funny to you?"

"I'm sorry," she says, stifling a laugh. "I just got this weird picture of you with, like, binoculars or something, spying on everyone in the village."

She laughs more.

So I laugh, too. And then I say, "And… if I *did* do that?"

"What?" Fi says. Then she tilts her head so she can see the coffee table past the easy chair. The binoculars sit right in the middle of the table - open, uncapped, and ready for use.

"You've gone all the way this time, haven't you, Lizzie?" she says.

"Just looking out the window," I say.

"With binoculars," she says, giving me a scoldy glare. "And now you're going to tell me they've been removing body parts in suitcases?"

"What!?" Nelly says, eyes wide open.

"She means *Rear Window*," I say.

Nelly looks confusedly at the back of my apartment, where there are no windows.

"*Rear Window* is the name of a movie, Fi says. "One that Lizzie's seen too many times."

"It's an old Alfred Hitchcock," I say. "I watch those once in a while."

"Once in a while?" Fi says.

"Okay, a lot."

"What's it about?" Nelly says.

"A guy is stuck in his apartment," I say.

"In his pajamas," Fi inserts, noting our matching attire.

"Yes, in his pajamas," I say. "Jimmy Stewart plays a man who has a broken leg, so he just sits in a chair all day, looking out his rear window at all the other apartment buildings that surround this big courtyard, watching the movements of the other tenants - including this one couple that's always fighting. Then, one day, the wife of that couple disappears, and her husband keeps taking his suitcase in and out of the apartment. And I think you can guess what's in the suitcase."

"You're not seriously suggesting my aunt..." Nelly says.

"No," Fi says. "All we're suggesting is that Lizzie has an active imagination, fueled by mystery novels and old movies."

"Still, that's a freaky sounding movie," Nelly says.

"We could watch it tonight," I say, before I recognize the obvious impropriety of the suggestion. "Or... not."

"Let's get back on track here, Lizzie," Fi says. "Do you have any actual evidence at all? Anything we can look at or touch?"

"Well, the note that appeared on Wanda's door," I say.

Nelly picks up her apron - which, of course, is actually

Wanda's apron. She unfurls it, and she pulls the note out of the pouch.

All three of us look at it together.

On Vacation
Back Next Week
- W. Beecher

"First of all," I say. "That's not her handwriting, is it, Nelly?"

"It doesn't look like it to me," Nelly says. "It's too stiff. Too something."

"Can we double-check it somehow?" Fi says. And I have to grin because finally she's actually, sort of, getting into this.

Nelly reaches back into the pouch of the apron and pulls out a bunch of small papers: a few recipes, a to-do list, a few of Wanda's 'notes to self.' She lays them out on the table.

"Okay, let's see what we have here," Fi says, leaning close. Her eyes dart back and forth between the two notes. After a moment, she says, "The first thing I notice is that the sign from the door is written in marker, whereas the other notes are all in pencil."

"Right. Good point," Nelly says.

"But that's just an observation," Fi says. "That's all we're doing here, just collecting observations. No conclusions yet."

"Sure," Nelly says. "So what else do you observe?"

"Well, as for the handwriting itself, the door sign has some similarities to the other writing, but it doesn't look as natural or effortless."

"I agree," Nelly says. "It's not free and easy - which is how Wanda really is.

"Right," I say. "When I look at this vacation note, I don't *see* Wanda, you know what I mean?"

"Exactly," Nelly says. "But when I look at these other notes, I *do* see her. I look at the page, I think, 'Oh - *Wanda.*"

"But Lizzie," Fi says. "What's the one thing I'm always

telling you about police work?"

"Hunches aren't evidence," I concede. "Feelings aren't proof."

"Exactly."

"But this is more than just a feeling," Nelly says. "The two notes really look different. Look at all these places where the ink gets wider, like the writer paused before making the next stroke. They actually had to think about it."

"Yeah," I say. "Wanda herself wouldn't have to pause to think about how she writes in her own handwriting, would she?"

"I'm not agreeing to anything yet," Fi says. "I'm just listening."

"So can we get a handwriting expert to compare the writing," Nelly says. "Would that be proof?"

"It would be interesting," Fi says. "But as far as the police are concerned, I wouldn't call it proof of anything."

"But it would have *some* significance, at least," I say.

"Yes, but..."

"So can you get it checked out?" I ask.

"You know my answer already, Lizzie," she says. "Before you submit evidence to a forensic expert, you need to be sure that it's worth the expert's time."

"Before we can prove it, we need to prove it," Nelly says. "Is that what you're actually telling us?"

"Pretty much," Fi says. "You need to see all this from the perspective of someone who doesn't believe you."

"Like you," I say, pouting a little.

"Like Occam's Razor," Fi says.

"That's a logic thing, right?" Nelly says. "I learned about it in college. *The simplest explanation is usually the best.* Is that it?"

"That's the one," I say.

"So what does Occam see when he looks at these notes?" Nelly asks Fi.

"To start with, we assume that the note from the door really was written by Wanda - since that explanation would make this whole thing simpler."

"Okay, but then why would the handwriting look different?" I say.

"They were written for different purposes. The note on the door wasn't an off-hand 'note to self' or a 'Gone to the bank, back in 5 minutes' kind of thing, like the other ones are. It's an official announcement for the general public, not just her regular customers. That's why it's more deliberate and more formal."

"I *guess*," Nelly says. "But… W. Beecher? Fi, who besides a British M.P. calls themself 'W.'?"

"I see your point," Fi says. "But remember, you don't have to convince me. You have to convince Occam. And since I'm Occam for the moment, I still don't really get why you'd question the note in the first place. Is there any way Wanda could have decided that since you were coming and knew how to run the shop, she'd take it as a chance to take a getaway vacation?"

"I don't know, *maybe*," Nelly says. "She knows I don't know how to run the shop even close to how she runs it. The only thing I make is muffins, and the only kind of muffin I'm actually good at making is blueberry. But no cakes. No pastries. Those are a big part of her sales, too. And now that the display shelves are basically empty, I'm not sure it even makes sense to open tomorrow. She had to know this would happen if she left me alone, and she would have given me more instructions when we emailed about me coming to visit."

"When was that?"

"Two days ago," Nelly says. "I emailed my aunt out of the blue and asked if I could come. She said 'sure,' so I drove up from Tennessee. Took me all day. And the only thing I heard from Wanda the whole time is an email I got in the middle of the night."

"What did it say?"

"Not much. It just had this messed up recipe."

"What do you mean, 'messed up'?" Fi says.

"It was for a baked dessert loaf we used to make together when I worked here a few years ago, but the directions were wrong. And not just 'minor typo' wrong. It felt like the recipe was wrong on purpose. I didn't make much of it at the time because I had no reason to. I just figured I'd see her soon enough and ask her what it was about. But when I got here, I came straight to the shop, and all I found was the note. I used my spare key to get inside, and then right after that, I ran into Lizzie."

"And you too decided together that your aunt was sending you a signal or something," Fi says.

"Kind of."

"And do you know that Lizzie is currently reading a mystery book where that exact thing happens?"

"No, but…"

"And you said that you went straight to shop this morning. So you're telling me that you're looking for your aunt, but you haven't actually been to her house yet?"

"No. But Lizzie has."

"Oh. Lizzie, please don't tell me you broke into her house like you did with the Muffin shop?"

"Of course not."

"But you tried."

"Kind of," I say.

"Well, did you find anything? Besides her cat, apparently."

"No."

"And has anything else actually happened around here in the meantime? I mean, *actually* happened?"

"Just… a lot of construction noise."

"From Devin doing his carpentry work at the entrance," Fi says.

"Yes, that. But also other noises from somewhere. I don't know where. The basement, I think."

"You *think*?" Fi says. "There's that 'think' word again."

"Well it's hard to tell," Nelly says. "Because when Devin gets quiet, the other banging stops."

"So Devin *is* the source of the noise."

"No! I mean, I don't..." Nelly says, dropping the 'think' entirely this time. "The banging from the basement, or wherever it's from, stops when Devin stops - like they're using the sounds of Devin's compressor and nail-thing to hide what *they're* doing."

"Okay," Fi says. "And that's all you have?"

"When you put it like that, it doesn't sound like much. But really, if you watch them like we've been watching them..."

Fi checks her watch. "Well, I can't. In fact, I really have to get home."

"You're just going to leave?" Nelly says.

"What else is there to do at this point?" Fi says. "You've called the police. Ramos is aware of the situation, and they're keeping an eye open. Julia is a good officer, and she's thorough. She won't just drop this."

"That's good," I say. "Let's just hope we're not too late."

Fi slips her work blazer back on and takes out her keys.

"Wait," I say. "Before you go, I want to check outside to make sure the coast is clear."

I walk to the window and look through the lace curtains.

Wanda's place is quiet and dark. But over at the discount store, Griff is standing in the doorway. And he's... just standing there. I grab the binoculars, to get a better look at his face. He keeps grimacing, and his eyes are going everywhere. What's he looking for?

"Guys, come over here," I say.

Nelly and Fi join me at the window, and we see Griff step outside his store and walk in front of the muffin shop. He takes a look inside.

Then he walks back into the discount store, and he stands in the picture window, looking out. His shoulders go up a little, and then they slump down in what looks like a deep sigh, and he starts chewing his nails.

I look up and down to check again for what he might possibly be looking for, but everything else on the street is quiet and normal.

Except, wait a minute, now a long black sedan glides down the street and stops in front of the bank. A man in a business suit gets out of the back seat, which tells me the car is being driven by a chauffeur of some kind. The business suit man is holding a package. It's a large manilla envelope, thick with documents. It looks important. A guard holds the door to the bank for him, and I can see in the shadows through that door that a woman in a pinstripe skirt and business jacket greets him. Then they all disappear inside together.

The front door swings closed, and all is quiet again.

"What's that about?" Nelly says.

"Seems like something to me," I say.

"Why?" Fi says. A high-level package delivered to the bank? Happens on a regular basis, I'm sure."

"So there's nothing to see here, folks - is that what you're telling us?" Nelly says.

Fi shrugs.

"Check that out, though," I say, because Griff is still in the discount store window.

We all look down at him together, and it's plain to see he's not bored and anxious any more. Instead, he's staring very hard at the black sedan with a look of eager anticipation.

And now the pinstripe suit woman returns. She opens the front door of the bank and holds it for the business suit man, who's no longer holding the package. He pauses to shake the woman's hand, and then he strides up to the sedan. He climbs in the back, and the vehicle glides away.

Griff tracks the sedan as it leaves. Then he turns and disappears into the shadows at the rear of the discount shop. And within one minute, the discount boys' old white van emerges from the alley, with Griff driving. Cory is in the passenger seat. We can all see that. But with my binoculars, I'm the only one who can see that the second row of seats is empty. No Nate.

"Okay, Fi," I say. "Tell me all that doesn't mean

something."

She nods. "I will admit it: that was interesting."

"That's all?" I say. "Just 'interesting'?"

"That's more than I usually say, isn't it?"

"I *guess*."

"Look, she says. "I do think you should continue to monitor the situation - which I'm guessing you were planning to do anyway, given the fact that you're both all cozied-up in your pajamas, with fleece blankets everywhere."

And now that Fi is noticing all the blankets, she also once again notices Powder curled up in the folds of SuperFuzz.

She looks at me.

"One cat!" I say. "Only one. And it's not even mine. It's Wanda's."

"And keeping in mind what I told you about me being a mandated reporter of crimes, do you have anything to say about *how* you came to have Wanda's cat?"

"Um..."

"Actually, let me stop you right there," Fi says. "And let's agree that you're going to eye on things tonight - but that's all you're going to do. No more break-ins."

"No," I say. "Of course not."

"I mean no break-ins *at all*," Fi adds. "No sort of break-ins that aren't really break-ins - at Wanda's house or the muffin shop or Dollar Discount or anywhere. I'll call you in the morning, unless you call me first, which we both know you probably will."

"I probably will," I admit.

"Fine. Just stay here, in this apartment, and have your slumber party. "

"That works for me," I say, because of course it does. "Nelly?"

"Works for me, too," she says. "I mean we're already..."

"Pajama-ed?" I say.

"Exactly," Nelly says. "We are thoroughly and completely pajama-ed."

After Fi leaves, Nelly and I settle in.

I make some microwave popcorn, and we take turns at the window looking for any movement or sounds from down on the street. But all we see is the soft, distant glow of a light on somewhere in the rear of the discount store - which for all we know is just a security light. Eventually, Nelly falls asleep on the couch, and I fall asleep in the easy chair.

And even though I'm sitting up, I sleep soundly. Deeply. Quietly.

No dreams that I can remember. No strange occurrences to disturb me.

Until the morning, that is.

Part Five - Freaky Friday

"*I deserve this,*" *Nate said, pacing back and forth.* "*You don't, but I do.*"

"*It's okay,*" *Wanda said.*

"*I should have known it would happen. Or something like it.*"

"*Probably,*" *she said.* "*But, Sweetheart, you need to settle.*"

He didn't settle.

"*I mean, I was never a partner to them,*" *he said.* "*I was a hired hand at best. And do you want to hear something funny? They never even told me how much they were going to pay me. Can you believe that! Would you take a job without even knowing how much they were going to pay you? It's obvious now that they were never going to pay me anything, ever. And now you and I are trapped here. It's my fault and I'm so sorry.*"

"*I know you are. But, really...*"

"*If I ever get out of this - if _we_ ever get out of this, that is - I promise I'll never do anything like it again,*" *Nate said.*

"*I know that,*" *Wanda said.* "*But listen to me. There will be time for promises later. Right now, we need to stay calm.*"

"*Yes,*" *he said.* "*You're right.*"

"*And, to be clear, we are going to get out of this.*"

"*How?*" *he said.* "*The door's completely blocked. We've tried a hundred times, and we got nowhere. They took my phone before they shut us in here. And when they saw you sending that last email to your niece just now, they took my laptop, too. We have no way of contacting anyone. There are no windows. There's no nothing.*"

"*Still,*" *she said, putting a hand on his shoulder.* "*It's going to be fine. Something good is going to happen before the end of this. I know it.*"

He took a big breath and then let it out slowly.

"*And it's not all that bad, is it?*" *she said.* "*They didn't tie us* up, which is good."

He shrugged. A good sign. A small one, but still it was something. She knew how afraid he was of the others. Bringing him around slowly was the only way.

"And we have each other to talk to. So that's good, too."

"Wow, you really know just the right thing to say sometimes, don't you?" he said. He was so much calmer than he had been even a few minutes ago. "I just wish I'd met you before all this. You could have talked me out of it, for sure."

"I'll be honest with you, Sweetheart," she said. "I wish that, too."

He smiled. Fully smiled. And he even laughed a little.

Down Comforter

I open my eyes to the soft glimmer of refracted sunlight through loops, diamonds, and flowers. I'm looking at the patterns on the white lace curtains, and my eye tracks the fine, delicate strands as they weave around each other.

It's beautiful. And interesting. Because why am I looking at the curtains in the front window of the living room when I just woke up in my bed?

Oh, right. I'm not in my bed. I'm in the easy chair.

Now I start to reorient myself, and I remember I'm not alone right now. I look back at Nelly, who's asleep on the couch.

She opens her eyes. Slowly.

She looks around. Now it's her turn to remember where she is and what she's doing here. I wait for her to figure that out - or at least most of it.

"Anything new?" she says, in a scratchy just-waking-up voice, as she sits up.

I push open the lace curtains just enough to get a view of the quiet street. Shops. Lantern street lights. Teabridge.

"Nothing."

"Good," Nelly says. "I *think*." She rubs her eyes and then stretches, rousing Powder from her spot curled up at the far end of the sofa.

As she reaches over to pet the cat, she notices her phone, poised on the edge of the coffee table. The screen is black, but the tiny indicator light in the corner is blinking.

She picks up the phone and clicks it fully on.

She takes a breath. "I have a message," she says.

"Oh?"

"It's..."

"It's what?" I say.

"It's from Aunt Wanda."

"You're kidding."

"No, I'm not. She sent it a few hours ago."

"In the middle of the night?"

"Yes," she says. "Right around three o'clock - the same time I got the email message the night before."

"Wow. Are you going to open it?" I ask her.

"Yeah - but I'm kinda scared."

"But you *are* going to open it," I say, trying to sound more hopeful than insistent.

She nods. Then she opens the email and stares at it.

Then she stares at it some more.

And each second that she remains quiet feels like an hour.

"Um… You know the rule about how if you start to say something, you have to finish it?" I say. "Does that apply to emails, too? I mean, I know she's your aunt, so I understand if you really don't want to read it. But..."

"It's okay," she says. "I'll read it."

She reads it…

"So glad you're looking after the store for me. I'm staying down in Brimfield at the cabin. Will send photos soon. Love, Auntie Wanda. PS - Don't forget to wash the down comforter that's folded up on the stairs at the shop."

"Okay," I say. "If Fi were here, she'd say this was good news, and that we can both now relax and think happy thoughts about Wanda sitting in an Adirondack chair on a pond in Brimfield, enjoying some well-deserved rest. But we're not thinking happy thoughts, are we?"

"No, we're not," Nelly says. "I'm not buying this at all. The email from the night before was weird, and this is twice as weird."

"Go ahead, then," I say, joining her on the couch. "Let's look at what's wrong with it."

"Plenty," Nelly says. "First of all, the message says 'down in Brimfield.' But Brimfield is west of us, not south. And second of all, Wanda doesn't have a cabin."

"Right. But could she have rented one?"

"Then why would she call it 'the' cabin? You call something 'the' when it's a specific thing - like, 'the cabin I always stay at.' Plus, this wouldn't make sense to anyone except you and maybe the woman who owns the yarn store downstairs, but Wanda doesn't own any down comforters. And she never would own one. Because what she really likes is..."

"Quilts," I say, remembering the beautiful ones I saw when I peeked through the front window at her house.

"You've got it," Nelly says.

"Whoa."

"I agree with your whoa."

We continue to stare at the email.

"The wording of this is so strange," she says. "'Comforter folded up on the stairs.' I don't know why, but that just strikes me as weird."

She leans forward and stares at the message on the screen even harder for several seconds, to no avail. Then she leans back and just kind of slumps. .

"You're hungry, aren't you?" I say.

"Sure," she says. "And thank you. Until you said that, I didn't realize just how hungry I am."

"It was easy to spot. The only times I've seen you the least bit discouraged is when you're hungry," I say. "Do you want some toast-logs?"

"Some...?"

"Toast-logs," I say, like it's a common term. However, since it's actually not a common term, but rather a term I invented myself yesterday, I explain. "Toast logs are like Yule Logs, except..."

"Made with toast?"

"Yes. They're my current favorite breakfast, aside from Wanda's muffins - or your muffins, for that matter. Would you like me to make you some?"

"You know something?" Nelly says. "This might be the craziest thing that I've said in the last few days, but yes. I would like a toast Yule-log. Very much, actually."

I go over to the kitchenette and turn on the kettle for tea, and I put four pieces of toast in the toaster oven. Then I check the dryer. Nelly's jeans that I washed and dried last night could use another five minutes, so I put the machine on the touch-up cycle. This way, they'll be nice and warm when she puts them on.

Nelly eats while lying back on the couch, with the plate on her stomach. She likes the food I made her, and she seems a little more relaxed now.

While I eat my own toast-logs and sip my tea, I stare again at the patterns in the lace curtain - just because I find it peaceful. I start at the upper right hand corner of the curtain and follow the outside fringe as it curls around itself, over and over, all the way down the frame to the lower right hand corner. Then I choose an individual strand of yarn as it weaves its way back up through the rectangles and the diamonds and the flowers.

Staring like this settles my mind. Clears it, even.

And in this clarity, a thought rises like a porpoise gliding to the surface from way down in the dark depths of the ocean. Or, for that matter, like a strand of yarn gliding up through lattice to the top of a white curtain.

"I've got it!" I say out loud.

"Mm?"

"I've got it," I say. "I figured it out."

"You figured out... what?"

"Everything," I say.

Nelly turns on the couch and props her head on her lower arm. She blinks her eyes. "Explain."

"They're planning to rob the bank!" I say.

"What? How do you know?"

"Well, I don't *know* - not for sure. But you saw the way Griff was acting last night when that black limousine-thing pulled up and dropped off that package."

"He was pretty curious."

"I would say he was more than curious," I say. "I'd say he was interested for a reason. Specifically, I think he wants to steal whatever that man deposited last night."

"Okay. But how? How is he planning to do that?"

"We've both noticed how Griff and his boys seem to be around all day, yet when you were working in Wanda's shop, you'd only see them out in the rear parking lot for brief stretches."

"That's true."

"And we practically never see them in the showroom part of their shop, right?" I say.

"Pretty much never," she says.

"Right. So if they've been around all this time, and they haven't been in the showroom or the back parking lot, then the only other place they could be is…"

"The basement!" she says. "They've been doing something in the basement this whole time."

"That's what I'm thinking," I say.

"What do you think they're doing in the basement?" she asks me. "You have a theory, don't you?"

"I do," I say. "I think they're trying to get into the bank from underneath somehow. Like, they're trying to tunnel into it. And the boxes they keep bringing in and out could be tools that they need, or they're getting rid of the dirt that they're tunneling through. This could be what Wanda's been trying to tell us in her email when she keeps finding excuses to write the word 'down.' As in, '*down* in Brimfield.' A '*down* comforter.' '*Down* on the stairs at the shop.'"

"And the only stairs in Wanda's shop lead…down," Nelly says.

"To the basement."

"But we checked the basement in her shop and we didn't find anything at all."

"That's true," I say. "But we never checked the basement of the discount store."

I watch her face as the truth of what I'm saying begins to

dawn on her.

She sits up, all the sudden.

"We have to do something!" she says.

"Okay. Good," I say. "What should we do?"

"Call someone. The police. Call this Officer Ramos person to tell her."

I grimace.

"What?" she says. "You think we still can't call her?"

"Not after we already called her. Because I hate to say it, but this still isn't proof of anything. It's just a theory. It's a good one, I think. But it's not proof. And it's not enough to take to the police."

"Can we at least take it to your sister?"

"We'd need something more," I say.

"Because she wouldn't believe it."

"The 'Fi' part of her might, possibly, believe it," I say. "Or at least she'd really enjoy laughing at me for telling it all to her. But the 'Ms. Fiona Groff Bradford, Licensed Forensic Psychologist' part of her would glare at me and tell me again to think like someone who doesn't believe me."

"Occam's Razor cuts again."

"Exactly."

"But you still say the 'Fi' part might, possibly, believe it?"

"Sure."

"So call the 'Fi' part of her. Now. Before she actually starts work."

I look at the old analog clock above the stove over in the kitchenette. Five forty-five. "Still too early," I say. "Her kids might be up, but she won't be - not for another hour."

"But this is an emergency. I mean, isn't it?"

"She won't see it that way."

"I'm sorry, Lizzie, but I can't wait anymore - not if Aunt Wanda is trapped in the basement right across the street. I can't just wait for someone else to like the idea. If Wanda's over there, and no one will help us get her out, then we'll just have to go do it."

"What would we do, specifically? Break into the discount store?"

"We start by going to Wanda's shop, just to get closer and see if the guys are around," Nelly says. "And if they're not there, then yes, maybe we can get into the discount store somehow, so that we can get down into their basement. You said it's been quiet there all night, right?"

"I didn't say *all* night. I can't vouch for the whole night because I haven't been awake that long."

"Still, it's quiet now," she says.

"Yes. It seems to be, anyway."

"So we can use the muffin shop as a hiding place while we check it out."

I see the look on her face - not just the eagerness, but the sadness underneath. And I understand why she can't wait anymore. If there's even a long-shot way for her to help her aunt, she's got to do it.

"Okay," I say.

"Okay?"

"Yes: okay. Let's go," I say. "Let's get dressed and go over there."

I take Nelly's jeans out of the dryer and toss them to her. Then I go into my bedroom to get dressed too. And I have to say that it feels strange to put on regular clothes after I've been in my pajamas so much lately. So I choose a casual outfit of jeans and a t-shirt, just to ease the shock to the system a little. And even then, I still feel like I'm preparing to go undercover as a normal person or something.

When we're all ready, we stand at the front door and take a deep breath together.

She nods to me, and then I nod to her.

Good. Here we go.

We slip downstairs, walking as lightly as we can until we get down to the foyer, where we stop to look outside and assess our next step. The street is still quiet, which is good because that probably means that no one else is awake. On the other hand, that's bad because if anyone *is* up, like one of the discount boys keeping a lookout, then we'll be really conspicuous walking around at this hour. No street commotion at all to give us cover.

But sometimes the only way to do something is to just do it.

So we do it.

We sprint across the street, staying side-by-side the whole time. Though Nelly could easily outrun me if she wanted, she doesn't, and I'm grateful for her small favor of not abandoning me.

From this angle on the street, I can see deep into the discount store window. And the further back I see, the darker and shadowier it gets. No movement. No sign of people.

We keep running until we get to Wanda's door. Nelly quickly unlocks it, we slip inside the shop, and she locks the door behind us right away.

We stop for a moment for a breath, taking advantage of the quiet safety. We listen for any sounds coming from next door, but nothing.

"The showroom of the discount store is empty, isn't it?" Nelly says. "You saw it, too, when we ran over."

"I did," I say. "But let's check the parking lot behind the building before we do anything else."

We go to the back of the shop, through the hallway that leads to the rear door, and we peer out. The only cars out there are my own car and the others belonging to the long-time tenants. Nothing strange or unusual. No old vans with dark windows.

Hm. Maybe the coast *is* clear.

Nelly pushes the back door open, and when we step outside, she heads right to the rear door of the discount store - which, whoa, is a little quick for me. I feel like we should still be checking things out a little more first. So I focus on the parking lot because, I don't know, I just have a feeling...

That...

Someone is here after all.

And I'm right: Nate is back over by the dumpster. We didn't see him at first because he's been pacing nervously, and he only comes into view after Nelly has started her break-in attempt.

He's waiting for Griff and Cory, no doubt - which is why he's been so focused on the alley and not the parking lot back here. But he sees me now. We're looking right at each other, in fact. I'm hoping that if I hold his gaze and don't flinch, he might somehow *not* notice Nelly just two feet away from me, trying to jimmy the lock on the back door of the store that he's been left to guard.

He still sees her, of course, despite my psychic mind trick. But he doesn't yell or scream. And he doesn't pick up a tire iron or some other weapon and come after us. Instead, he looks right back at me with an urgency, like he's telling me to get Nelly to stop what she's doing and just get out of here.

In short, he's trying to help us.

And boy, that does not make much sense.

But this is not the time to figure it out. So I grab the back of Nelly's t-shirt. She turns around and gets a jolt when she sees Nate all at once, right here.

To keep her calm, I say, "Come on," under my breath. I guide her back to the rear door of Wanda's. We even walk backwards, slowly, keeping our eye on Nate the whole time. And am I seeing this right? He nods slightly, as if to say, 'Yes - keep going. Get away, for your own sake.'

And now we hear a vehicle coming up the alley way, grinding and rumbling. Nelly and I drop caution and dive back into the rear of the muffin shop and then crawl down the hallway, far enough so that we're hidden from anyone outside.

From the safety of these shadows, I look back through the window as the old white van arrives.

When Griff and Cory get out, we see Nate take a big breath, building up his courage for the encounter.

Griff walks right up to him, no doubt to ask if anything unusual happened when they were gone. And again, to our surprise, Nate shrugs and shakes his head 'no' - even though, obviously, he just caught Nelly and me trying to break into their store. He then stammers through a clumsy version of 'Nothing to see here, Griff' that somehow works. It probably helps that they have other things on their mind besides the verbal tics of their flakey junior member. Griff brushes past him and heads in through the rear door of their store - to resume his dark work, no doubt. Cory follows him, with Nate trailing behind.

A few feet before he gets to the door, Nate hesitates a moment, and I get a full view of his face right in the back window.

And he looks freaked out, shell-shocked, and just really, really scared. And I feel like, for the first time, I'm seeing the kind of person he really is: a nice guy trapped in a mess that's too hard for him to handle. So he puts his head down and follows the others into the rear of the discount store.

And that's it. They're gone.

Crisis averted, thanks to Nate.

And I said a moment ago that it's surprising that Nate helped us. But maybe by this point it shouldn't be. He's always seemed different than the others. He's always been the naive outsider. The one they leave behind to watch over things at night.

"They don't treat him very well, do they?" Nelly says, reading my thoughts.

"No, they don't. They make him do the things they don't want to do, like bringing the heavy boxes up from the basement. I think they even make him stay here all night to watch over the store."

"Or maybe to watch over Wanda," Nelly says. "I mean, if she *is* in their basement, they'd want someone keeping an eye on her."

"That would explain why the two emails from Wanda this

week came at three o'clock in the morning," I say. "If she was alone with Nate, she must have convinced him to let her write to you."

"Oh my gosh, I can just picture Nate and her together in the middle of the night, when he's tired and feeling guilty and scared about the robbery. And the only person he has to talk to is Wanda herself, the nicest person he's ever going to meet. It's a wonder he hasn't given up the whole thing completely. "

"The others have a hold on him, somehow," I say. "I just know it. Whether they're bribing him or blackmailing him or just threatening him, it's definitely something. I wouldn't want to cross Cory, that's for sure. Not without going into witness protection."

"Speaking of edgy," Nelly says. "Griff was *really* edgy last night when he was spying on the people at the bank - even more than usual. So why? What's changed?"

"Maybe he's finally realizing that their plan to rob the bank is just a really, really bad one," I say. "I mean, right? If they're trying to tunnel in through the basement, that's just wrong on so many levels. The walls have to be way too reinforced to penetrate. And if they miraculously get through somehow, the bank has surveillance cameras everywhere. However much those guys want their plan to work, deep down they have to know it never will."

"But they're doing it anyway," she says. "They're in too deep to pull out now, so they're going ahead with it. But because it's such a bad plan…"

"The closer they get to zero hour, the more anxious they become."

"And are you thinking what I'm thinking?"

"Are you thinking that zero hour is sometime today?" I say.

"Yes."

"Then I'm thinking what you're thinking. This is supposed to be Devin's last day working for them, and Griff promised Officer Ramos he'd be out of there by five o'clock."

"So five o'clock is zero hour."

"It makes sense," I say. "The bank closes at five. Everything else on that block would be closed. Devin would be gone. Nothing and no one would be left in Bank Row except them and their devious plan."

"And Wanda," Nelly says. "If she really is tied up in their basement, I don't know what they'll do with her once they rob the bank. But they're not going to just let her go."

"That's for sure," I say.

"So *now* can we call your sister? It's six thirty."

"I think we'd better," I say. "I suddenly feel like there's a big hourglass on the table that's about to run out of sand."

"Like in *The Wizard of Oz*?"

"Exactly!" I say. "That's exactly what I mean."

I dial Fi's number, and she picks up on the first ring.

"I wonder who this is," she says.

"Did I wake you?"

"I *wish*," she says. "Ella's been coughing all night. I've been up since three."

"Well, at least you're alert," I say, "because I want to give you an update. Are you ready?"

"I'm sitting up in bed with my third cup of coffee, hoping this one will do the trick. So if you have some news to tell me, now's as good a time as any."

"It's not news, actually. It's more of a theory."

"And what do we keep saying about theories?"

"I know, but just listen. We've figured out the whole thing," I say. "The discount boys are planning to rob the bank."

"What?"

"Just what I said," I tell her. "They're going to rob the bank. I mean, you saw how Griff was acting when that sedan was outside the bank last night, right?"

"Well, yes - but..."

"You said yourself that it was 'interesting.'"

"That's all I said, and it's still all I say. Because how are they going to do this in the first place?" she says. "Are they just going to walk into the bank and tell them, 'Give me the package that got delivered here yesterday?'?"

"No. They're going to rob the safe by tunneling into it from underneath."

"Tunneling."

"Yes."

"From underneath."

"Yes," I say. "And I know you think it's crazy, but that's why they've been making so much construction noise all week."

"You mean the work the Wahl kid was doing?"

"No. Devin's carpentry stuff is just a distraction to cover up for the real work they're doing in the basement. And Wanda must have caught them at it somehow, so they've kidnapped her. Or worse."

"Well, this is quite a story, Lizzie," she says. "I'm not sure it even rises to the level of a theory, but just to be clear, either way, it's still not proof."

"But we got a new email."

"From Wanda?"

"Yeah. She says she's staying at a cabin in Brimfield."

"Okay," she says. "I know you're going to say you don't believe it, so say it."

"Well, I *don't* believe it," I say. "The email doesn't make sense. And we think she wrote it that way on purpose because she's in trouble. See? She can't tell us outright, so she's been filling her messages to us with clues. I'll show it to you. It explains everything. When you read it, tell me it isn't proof enough, even for you."

Nelly sends Fi the email from her phone.

When I know that Fi has received it, I give her a few moments to read. And when I can't wait any longer, I break in. "Do you see what I mean?"

"What, exactly, am I supposed to see?" Fi says. "She's at her cabin."

"No, that's just the point. She doesn't have a cabin. And you don't drive 'down' to Brimfield from where we are; you drive *over* to it. You drive west. And there's no comforters folded up 'down' on the stairs, because Wanda doesn't like comforters - she likes quilts. So tell me all this still isn't enough for you to think Wanda is in their basement. *Down* in their basement, to be specific."

"I'm sorry, Lizzie, but the most generous thing I could call it - and this is being really generous - is a lead."

"Fine. It's a lead," I say. "So follow it."

"I can't do that," she says. "I'm not a detective."

"Well someone has to!" I say. "The discount boys are going to make their move when the bank closes at five o'clock today. We just know it. If we don't get Wanda out by then, they could get away, and they could take her with them. Or worse."

"Okay, listen," Fi says. "I'll talk to Ramos. I'll see if she's got anything new on her end."

"And show her the new email," Nelly says.

"If you insist. But she'll most likely take it at face value and assume Wanda is on vacation at a cabin in Brimfield. Case closed."

"But she could check the Dollar Discount basement, right? If there's nothing there, then *that's* your case closed."

"She can't force her way into someone's basement without a warrant. We talked about this already."

"But can she at least talk to them again?" I tell her.

"I suppose I could nudge her in that direction," Fi says, reluctantly.

"You have to do more than nudge," I say. "You have to make sure she comes. We've got to get Wanda out of there before five o'clock today. Promise me you'll make that happen."

"I'll make a deal with you," Fi says. "I'll promise to get Ramos to come talk to them before five o'clock today, if you promise not to do anything crazy in the meantime."

"Okay, sure. I promise. But we can still keep an eye on things, right? No harm in looking."

"You look, but you don't touch," she says. "Understand? Do we have a deal?"

I put my hand over the phone's microphone and I turn to Nelly, who's been listening the whole time.

"It's not everything we want, but it's something," I say to her. "What do you say?"

Nelly nods, and I get back on the line.

"We have a deal," I tell her. "Have a good day, Sis. And thanks."

I hang up and look to Nelly again. "So that's it. Something's definitely going to happen today."

"That's good," she says. "But it's so hard thinking that Wanda's right across the street, somewhere in their basement. I feel like I should be there with her, somehow."

""So...." I say. "Let's open the shop."

"The muffin shop?"

"Absolutely," I say, "If you think about it, we really have to do it. It's the best way for us to keep an eye on the discount boys, because if the shop is open as usual, they'll be less likely to think that we're onto them."

"Except what do we sell? We don't have any flour left to make more blueberry muffins."

"I could make toast," I say. "That would at least give people something to have with their coffee. And for a special, we could sell the toast logs, like I made for you this morning."

"Toast logs?" Nelly says, laughing. "You're suggesting we actually sell those?"

"You liked them, didn't you?"

"Better than I thought I would, actually," she says. "But we don't have any bread to make it with, and I don't know how to bake it - not to bakery standards, anyway."

"I could make some in my bread machine," I say. "How much do we need? A couple of loaves?"

"A couple of loaves?" she says. "Try a couple of dozen.

Wanda gets Leighton customers on Friday. During her peak time, she's got a steady line. We could have a hundred by noontime, easy. Sometimes double that. I mean, I'm not saying they'll all switch from muffins to toast in one day, but if we're going to do this, we have to be prepared."

"Okay, then I'll get some bread at the convenience store," I say. "I'll buy all the bread I can."

"And then you'll come back and help me, right? I mean, please say you're going to help me."

"At this point," I say, "I'm all in."

She smiles. "Me, too."

I call the main number at work, to tell them I'm taking a personal day. I'll check my emails later this morning, just to stay in touch. But for now, the task at hand is clear, and it's right here in Teabridge Village.

Toast Logs

We both get dressed, and we walk down to Wanda's. The shop inside feels warm and familiar this morning, with its comfy furniture and the earth-tone decor. This is Wanda's place: she deserves to be here.

We do a quick check of the rear door. Everything's settled and quiet. So Nelly starts making the coffee, and I head to the convenience store.

There's a strange mood to the Village this morning, but I can't exactly say why. I mean, passing by the Dollar Discount store is always strange these days, of course, but no one's in the showroom. I don't hear any strange noises. And the weather isn't doing any of the unusual Edicom Valley things it does sometimes.

But maybe the thing that's different is... me. *I* feel different. I'm on a mission, after all. You could even say it was a caper. And the world's going to look different to you when you're on a caper, isn't it?

I enter the convenience store. Helen's been open for at least a half hour, selling newspapers and to-go coffees. She's stocking tuna in the middle aisle when I say, "Hi Helen. I need bread."

She points to the bread section while she continues working.

"No - um, actually I need a *lot* of bread," I say. And now she stops working and looks at me, trying to figure out the curious thing I've just said.

"You get your deliveries today, don't you?" I ask her. "I've seen the truck here on Fridays. He delivers whole racks, right?

"He's been here already," she says.

"Can I buy one?"

"You mean one of the loaves? Sure."

"No. I mean one of the racks," I say.

"A whole rack?"

"Is that possible?"

"If I had an extra rack to sell you, I'd be happy to do it," she says. "But the two he delivered need to last all weekend. Bread is a staple item, and customers don't like it when we run out of staples."

I get where she's coming from, because it's a convenience store, after all. But I need to make this happen, so I go with a deeper appeal.

"You know Wanda?" I say.

"From the muffin shop?" Helen says. "Of course."

"You two get along, right? As fellow merchants in the village, you look after each other?"

"We do," Helen says. She's now completely stopped what she's doing, and she's looking right at me. "Wanda's helped me many times."

"Well, she hasn't been around for a few days," I say. "And I don't know how to explain it in sixty seconds or less, at least not in any way that would make sense, but..."

"But what?"

"We're just trying to find her, and believe it or not, if you sell us all the bread you possibly can, it will help."

She looks harder at me, deciding whether to believe me.

"Take half a rack," she says. "Will that help you for the time being?"

"Yes," I say. "Thank you."

"I'll call the distributor. If I can get another delivery today, I'll send more over."

"Wow," I say. "Thank you."

I go to the storage room in the back. Helen's assistant Mike puts five bags of bread in a big green garbage bag, simply because there's nothing else big enough to carry them.

On the way back out, I also buy as much butter as Helen will sell me, along with some jars of jams she has on special display on the counter.

So now I really have a lot of stuff.

Mike helps me tote it all back down the street to the muffin shop. I thank him, and then I hold up the provisions for Nelly to see.

"How many loaves did you get?" she says.

"Five. Twenty slices per loaf equals ten servings per loaf. So we have toast for the first fifty customers. Helen says she'll send more bread later, if they can get it."

"Nice," Nelly says. "Alright, let's get going."

The coffee is already brewing, so Nelly turns the sign on the door from 'Closed' to 'Open.'

Then I make another sign:

Today's Special: Toast
Served with your choice of butter or jam.
Or choose our deluxe Toast-log.

The first customer who comes in is a businessman on his way into work. I fill his travel mug with coffee and wait while he squints at the sign.

"Alright, why not?" he says. "I'll take an order of toast, to go."

"Can I interest you in our deluxe toast-log?" I say, proudly glancing down at my sign.

"A little too rich for my blood," he says.

"Fair enough," I say.

Luckily, two slices of toast fit in the same to-go bags Wanda uses for the muffins - which is good, because I'm surprised by how much toast people order as the morning rush gets going. And a few regulars do take me up on the toast-log. I watch them sitting at the cafe tables, eyeing the logs curiously, poking at them cautiously. Then they take a bite and smile: not bad after all.

Whenever things slow down enough for one of us to get away, we take turns finding an excuse to throw something away in the dumpster behind the building, just to see what's going on back there. And nearly every time, we run into Griff or Cory, or both. And nearly every time, they look surprised to see us - and frustrated, which is fine with us. Anything that slows them down makes it even more likely they'll botch their awful plan.

After one of her trips to the rear lot, Nelly casually walks behind the counter and stands close to me.

"I just saw Griff heading for his truck," she says under her breath. "But when he heard me come out, he threw his hands up in a huff and walked back into his store. Our being here in the shop is totally preventing them from doing something."

She's got a mischievous sparkle in her eye.

"I see that look," I say. "You've got an idea, don't you?"

"I do."

"Alright, let's just get through the morning rush, and then you can tell me whatever ingenious plan you're cooking up."

We get back to work, falling into the flow and rhythm of a muffin shop on an average Friday morning. It's *not* an average Friday morning, of course. But for a few nice hours, it feels like it.

Just after nine o'clock, Mike brings over a few more loaves of bread from the convenience store.

"Thanks," Nelly says. "And thank Helen, too. And let her know this should do it for us. We're almost through the busiest time, and we're still holding on. You guys really helped us a lot."

By ten-thirty, things finally do settle down, and we have some time to breathe. Nelly and I sit at one of the tables by the window and have some coffee with toast.

Now that we have a moment, I lean in close.

"Okay, what's this idea you have?" I ask her.

"Well, you've noticed that they keep trying to leave, right? But then they see us and they *don't* leave - like they're afraid to leave their place unattended. So should we lay low for a while? Stop interrupting them? Because if they do leave, maybe we can get into their shop and into their basement - and hopefully find Wanda."

"But we promised Fi that we'd wait," I say. "That was the deal: she gets Ramos to come by today, and we lay low. I don't want to break my promise."

"I don't want to break it either," she says. "But if the discount boys leave, that opens up an opportunity we didn't know we'd have."

"This is dicey," I say. "For one thing, if we did sneak in there - and I'm *not* saying that we're going to - we'd have to be absolutely sure they've all left. All three of them - even Nate. And how are we even going to get in there? If they leave, they're going to lock up."

"Does your friend Devin have a key?" she says.

"I doubt it. He really doesn't do much for them except stand out front and make a lot of noise," I say. "They have no reason to give him a key. If they're really kidnappers and wannabe bank robbers, they wouldn't give a key to anyone."

"But Devin is a carpenter," she says. "He could just take the front door off its hinges, and no pedestrians passing by would look twice and think he's breaking in, because he's been out there doing construction all week."

"Maybe," I say. I look out the window to see that, yes, Devin's van is out there. So he's started his work for the day.

But wait - what's this?

I also see, across the street... wait for it... Aaron.

And Ashley.

Ugh.

They're walking up the street, passing the yarn shop as we speak.

What are they doing here, and why are they doing it?

Unfortunately, I know the answer. I don't want to know it, but I do: Aaron and Ashley are looking for me because he's worried.

And now they've passed Yarned and they're headed for the door to my apartment building.

No.

No, no, no, no, no.

"Who's that?" Nelly says, seeing the completely bugged-out look on my face.

"It's my ex-boyfriend Aaron and his new girlfriend Ashley," I say. "He's checking on me. I took a personal day today - *one* single personal day - and he's rushed over here to rescue me from whatever dastardly fate he assumes I'm facing."

"And he brought his new girlfriend to do *that*?" Nelly says.

"She works for TechTile, too. They're traveling partners. Actually, they're pretty much always together. "

"It still seems a little loaded that he would bring her."

"It's plenty loaded," I say.

"If we stay here in the muffin shop, will they just leave?"

"He doesn't give up that easy, unfortunately. And look - oh, gosh - now he's jiggling the door to my building. I better go over there."

I'm so tense when I stand up that the chair makes a grinding sound as I push it back behind me.

"Do you want me to give you space?" Nelly says. "Or do you want me to..."

"I want you to come with me," I say. Definitively.

She joins me at the door, and we take a moment to make sure the shop is okay. It is. The customers here now are regulars, settled in with their laptops. They won't need anything for a while, and they're not going to steal anything if we leave them here.

So I step outside, and I almost forget to hold the door for Nelly behind me, because all I can think about - all I can *see* - is Aaron and Ashley across the street.

I'm in a roiled-up state of mind. I know I am. But what can I do?

Nelly stands beside me. With me. And for that matter, Devin is right nearby, too - up on his ladder here on the sidewalk, poised with a hammer in his hand. He's stopped working, and he's looking at me. Then he looks across the street at what I'm looking at.

And I suppose it's his right to look wherever he wants, and I'm really grateful for the supportive smile he gives me - but does everyone have to know about this?

I cross the street without looking both ways. Nelly rushes behind me, grabbing my shirt to hold me back as a quiet electric car does, in fact, pass right where my next step would have been.

Aaron sees me, and his face lights up. "Eliza!"

"Shh," I say. "Shh. I'm coming."

And now Ashley sees me too. Her face does not light up, however.

We get across, but I don't meet them at the door to my building. Instead, I stand in front of Yarned, and I nod to them to come over. Actively. Exaggeratedly. *Come on.*

Aaron approaches - a bit confused, but happy to see me. "Eliza, what's going on?" he says, still a few feet away.

"I was just about to ask you the same question," I say. "And could you keep it down, please? We're trying to..."

"You're trying to what?" he says.

"Alright, fine," I say. "I'll tell you." When he's close enough, I try to pull him into the yarn shop, and he insists on holding the door for me, Nelly, and then finally Ashley, who takes several labored steps to follow behind.

We sort ourselves out enough to gather around a display of felted animals in the front window.

"Eliza, I'm glad you're okay," Aaron says. "I was worried about you. First you leave work early yesterday - which you pretty much never do. And then you call in sick today, which you definitely never do."

"I didn't call in sick," I say. "I took a personal day."

"Why?"

"Why?" I echo. "What part of 'personal' day do you not understand? Hint: consider the 'personal' part of it."

And, ugh, I know I'm not being very nice to him, so I say, "I'm sorry. It's just that we're trying to do something here.

Something important."

"Oh?" Aaron says - leaning toward me, just a little too excited.

But I can't tell him what I'm doing. I mean, I can't, right? Right?

"I'm just... helping Nelly with the muffin shop," I say. "While her aunt's away."

Yeah - that's it. That's what I'm doing. And he'll buy it. Of course he'll buy it.

But no. Of course he's not buying it. In fact, he's smirking at me.

So, just to look at something else besides his piercing eyes, I stare out the window.

At... Devin.

He's off his ladder. He's put his hammer in his belt. And he's right now walking across the street towards us. What is he doing? I don't know.

I close my eyes to wish it all away.

But it doesn't work, because when I open them, Devin is entering the yarn shop in his work boots, Carhartts, and tool belt - looking every bit the contractor he is. And still, bless his heart, he's trying to look casual, as though he was halfway through hammering a nail into the side of the discount store when he suddenly had an uncontrollable urge to shop for yarn.

"Hi," he says to me. But, inevitably, to everyone. "Just came to make sure everything is okay here."

But that's not exactly true, is it? Because I know why he's come here. He saw Aaron, dressed to the nines in his business suit, and he got jealous. And now Devin is even tucking in his work shirt and straightening his toolbelt. His version of gussying himself up, I guess.

So I kind of slap his arm, to get him to stop. Not in a mean way - but more in the way that... well, there's no other way to say this: I do it in the playfully teasing way that people use when their romantic partner is embarrassing them. And *why* do I do this, even though Devin is obviously, in no way, my romantic partner?

I don't know.

But Aaron sees it and smiles a little. Everyone sees it, I'm sure. Ashley is smiling, too - though her smile is a little triumphant. I'm sure Nelly is smiling as well, though I can't bring myself to look over at her.

Aaron, ever the magnanimous one, breaks the awkward silence for everyone's benefit. "Nice to meet you," he says to Devin. "My name's Aaron."

Devin nods and shakes his hand. "Devin Wahl. Contractor."

"So I noticed."

"And this is Ashley," Aaron says. Ashley nods, but she doesn't offer her hand. She's feeling out of place, of course, and why wouldn't she? I kind of even, sort of, feel bad for her.

"Listen, Devin," Aaron says. "Is something going on here? Lizzie won't tell me."

And - wow - Aaron really can win people over in a heartbeat: Devin drops any jealousy he was feeling and leans toward him. "You bet there is," he says. "It's those guys in the new store across the street. I mean, that's what you think too. Right, Lizzie?"

"Hold on a second," I say, because all this is, like, *whoa*.

"Well, why not tell him?" Nelly says. "He's probably guessed half of it already."

"But..." I stammer.

"Think about it: Devin's already pretty much involved in it with us," she says. "And as for Aaron here, do you trust them?"

The truth is, I do trust him. I mean, he never cheated on me when we were together. He never lied to me. But, my gosh.

"Is the whole world really going to get involved here?" I say. "Hey - while we're at it, Cynthia is here, too. She's the owner of this shop we're hiding in right now, so we might as well let her join in. And she's not doing anything at the moment, aside from eavesdropping on every word we're saying while pretending to organize the skeins in that side display."

And, wouldn't you know it, Cynthia takes my extremely brief glance at her as a full invitation to come over to us.

"What are you up to?" Cynthia says. "It's Wanda, isn't it? Something's happened to Wanda."

"No!" I say. Then I add, a little defeated, "Maybe."

"Well, I want to help," she says.

"Why? You don't even like Wanda," I say. "You're always saying..."

"I'm always saying nothing of any importance," Cynthia interrupts. "I'm jealous of Wanda owning a muffin shop, just like she's jealous of me owning a yarn shop. But if she's in trouble, that's different. She'd do the same for me, and she wouldn't have waited three days to find out if I was okay. That's for sure."

"Three days?" I say.

"I know exactly how long she's been missing." she says. "I see everything from this window, and I've been fretting about her all week."

"You didn't look too fretful when you cozied up to the discount store guys just two days ago."

"I didn't cozy up to anyone. I had a bad feeling about them from the moment they pulled in, and I wanted to see if I was right. And I was right, wasn't I?"

"Apparently," I say.

"So tell me what's going on."

"Tell all of us," Aaron says.

I'm cornered. I shrug. I nod.

Cynthia glances around her store to see that no one else is here at the moment except us. Then she reaches over, clicks the lock on the front door, and turns her 'Open' sign to 'Closed.

Alright, then.

"Nelly, I say. "If we're doing this, we're doing it together."

"Fine with me," Nelly says. "Should I go first?"

"Go first," I say.

"Okay. Just to bring everyone up to speed, my aunt Wanda has been missing for three days now," she says. "I won't get into all the gritty details, but aside from a few very suspicious emails, she hasn't been seen or heard from since the discount store boys arrived. In a nutshell, we think they're planning to rob the bank when it closes at five o'clock today, and we think Wanda found out about it, so they kidnapped her and are holding her in their basement."

I'd wondered how much Nelly was going to share with them, and the answer is... everything. She's sharing everything with them.

Devin is nodding, because everything he's suspected all week is being confirmed.

Aaron is not nodding, however. He's puzzled.

"The bank isn't closing at five today," he says. "They're closing early - at one o'clock."

"Wait, what?" Devin says. "Why would they close early on payday?"

"They're merging a Leighton branch with this one, shifting that business over here," Aaron says. "The staff will all be gone this afternoon so that they can go clear out the other branch."

"How do you know this?" Nelly says.

"The company that Ashley, Eliza, and I work at banks with them. I know you don't deal with office finances, Eliza, but I assumed you at least heard that news. It's kind of a big deal, actually, and you live right here on this street. Did you notice any unusual activity at this branch the past few days?"

"Actually, we did notice something," Nelly says. "A guy dropped off an important looking package last night. But we didn't know what it meant."

"It means their merger plans are on track," Aaron says. "Which means they're definitely closing at one today."

"So we don't have all day to deal with this, like we thought," I say.

"Not at all," Aaron says. "It's ten-thirty now. We have three hours."

"Three hours at the *most*," Nelly says. "Because if you ask me, we need to stop this before it happens - not while it's happening. Or worse: after it's too late."

"Alright, let me call my sister," I say.

"Good idea," Nelly says. "Tell her to send the police. Tell her to send the cavalry, for that matter. Send everyone."

I call Fi. There's no answer, so I leave a voicemail. "Fiona," I say, using her full name, so that she knows I'm serious. "It's Eliza. I know I promised you that Nelly and I would lay low until the end of the day, but things have changed. So..."

Before I say my next sentence, I put my hand over my phone. I look at Nelly. "Are you sure?" I ask her.

"I'm sure," she says. "I can't wait anymore. I'm sorry if this pits you against your sister."

"It's alright," I say to her. "She'll be mad at first, but if she were in my position, she'd do the same thing."

I finish the message: "We have to act as soon as possible. In other words, right now. Please call me back. Or better yet, come as soon as you can - and Officer Ramos, too. Love you. Lizzie."

I hang up, and I turn to everyone.

And they're all... looking... at me. Which is weird enough, and then they start talking to me, too.

"We have to get inside the discount store, and we have to do it now, right?" Nelly says.

And Devin adds, "But how?" - like I'm the one who's going to guide us all in figuring this out.

Aaron's looking at me with the same expression. So is Ashley. And Cynthia.

Why are they looking at me like I'm the leader? I don't know.

My usual response when I'm put on the spot like this is to

just slink back out of the limelight and wait for everyone else to move on - which they always do.

But no one is showing any signs of moving on at the moment.

And actually - and this is very, very strange, at least to me - I do know what we all should do.

Or at least I have an idea.

The Plan

"Nelly is right," I say. "We need to get inside the store somehow. The boys have been in and out of the back door all day, and they show no signs of letting up, or of leaving. So we'll probably have to go through the front door somehow, which is locked, no doubt."

"I can handle that part," Devin says, tapping his tool belt.

"Yeah, we thought you might be able to," Nelly says.

"Okay, but we need a distraction," I say. "Even if you have your compressor going full blast, we can't risk them hearing you."

"We'll do that," someone says. "We'll be the distraction."

But *who* said it? Ashley? No. Couldn't have been.

But… yes. It *was* Ashley. Those are the first words she's said this whole time, and I have to admit, I admire her for joining in even though she doesn't really have a stake in this besides through Aaron. Still, she's pitching in. Lending a hand. Being a team player.

"Thank you," I say to her. "Any ideas as to how you might create that distraction?"

"Do they sell clothing?"

"They sell flannel shirts," I say.

"Of course you'd notice the flannel," Aaron says, smirking at me. And I hope for fifty-eight thousand reasons he's not being flirtatious.

Just to be sure, I put him in his place. "*Itchy* shirts, to be specific," I say, glaring.

"We know some distributors through TechTile," Ashley says, getting us back on track. "We could ask one of them to make a sales call or something."

"Good idea," Aaron says. "The local guy is a friend of mine. I bet we could even borrow his van. That way we'd be the ones making the sales call."

"Alright, so while Devin breaks into the front door, you two make your fake sales call in the parking lot behind Bank Row," I say. "But if we're going to be spread out like this, with people coming from different directions, we need a way to keep in touch."

"A virtual meeting app where we can see and talk to each other?" Nelly says.

"Exactly," I say. "There's an open source version you can all connect to now. We use it at work sometimes."

"Yes," I say. "And I'll map it all out, so that we're all absolutely clear. Cynthia, do you have some paper?"

"Right here," she says.

We gather at the long table in the center of the shop where Cynthia gives knitting lessons. She hands me a large sheet of thin gray paper from the roll she uses to sketch out projects.

I spread out the sheet and draw a crude map of this end of the street.

"Okay, so… here's Bank Row across the street," I say. I sketch a long rectangle and then divide it into boxes to indicate each storefront.

"Behind Bank Row is the parking lot," I continue. "The alley near the financial advisors is the main entrance, but there's a second entrance on the far side of the tile store. It's small and tucked away, so the dollar store boys probably don't even know about it. But we'll use that to our advantage by having you come through that way."

"Got it," Ashley says. "It makes sense when I see the map."

"I'm glad," I say. "But the back doors of the stores still won't make sense, even after I add them. It's surprisingly confusing back there. So as much as possible, lure the boys away from those doors. Get them as far away from the building as you can. That way, even if they do hear Devine, at least we can warn him that they're coming."

Now I draw two letter 'A's', for Aaron and Ashley, along with an arrow indicating their path starting at the far entrance to the parking lot. "You two will pull in through here. And when you do, block that entrance with your vehicle, so they can't get their van out. Sound good?"

Ashley and Aaron look at each other and nod. "Got it, boss," she says.

"Alright, next up we have Nelly."

"Here and ready," Nelly says.

"I'm thinking you should be stationed in your aunt's shop. You're the fastest runner here, so you're the best one to keep an eye on both Devin through the front door and on Aaron and Ashley with the discount boys in the rear. You can shuttle back and forth, running between the two doors. Plus, you'll be right down there close to everything, ready to help wherever it might be needed. If Devin does find Wanda, I don't think I could hold you back from running straight to her, and I wouldn't want to try. So be ready for that, actually."

"Works for me," she says.

"Good," I say. "Next is Cynthia."

I turn to her. "Are you really in on this? Because it's okay if you've..."

"I haven't changed my mind, and I'm not going to change it," Cynthia says. "If you have an idea for me, tell me what it is."

"I think you should stay right here in Yarned, actually," I say. "Your front window has a perfect view of three of our key areas of interest: the alleyway, the discount store, and the muffin shop. Beyond that, I'd give you the same instructions as Nelly: be ready."

"I'll be ready," she says, surprisingly calm.

"Then that brings us to you, Devin. Your instructions are simple, but that doesn't mean they're easy: get through the front door of the discount store somehow. Take it off its hinges, or whatever you have to do. Are those steel-toed boots you're wearing?"

"Sure," he says.

"Good. If things get desperate, kick your way through the

window."

"I'm doing all this alone?"

"Well, sort of. But you'll have your phone on the whole time, linked in to the conference app. You have a pouch on your toolbelt for your phone, right?"

"Yes," he says. "Right here." He slides the phone into the slot, with the camera facing forward.

"Perfect," I say. "Whatever you see, we'll see. And if you get in trouble at all, we'll know it right away, and we'll come running from all directions: Nelly from next door, Cynthia from here across the street, and Ashley and Aaron from the rear."

Devin smiles, reassured by the image of us all coming together like that. "And you?" he says. "Where are you going to be during all this?"

They're looking at me, like, *did you just write yourself out of this story?*

Did you just come up with a great plan involving all these great people - yet somehow not include yourself?

No, I didn't. Far from it, actually.

"I'll be up in my apartment," I say, "sitting in my easy chair."

This gets a big laugh from everyone.

But the thing is...

"I'm not kidding," I say. "I'll have a view of the whole street from up there, and I'll keep an eye on all of you through the conferencing app, which I'll bring up on my big laptop, with all your feeds on the screen at once."

"Actually, that makes sense," Ashley says, still laughing a little - but now with a hint of admiration. "The brains of the operation in 'command central.'"

"Alright, boss," Aaron says. "What's our next step? What do we need? And when do we start?"

I recognize those questions as the three 'momentum starters,' straight from the most recent TechTile motivational seminar. Yes, Aaron - I pay attention to those things.

I'm an introvert. I pay attention to everything.

"Next step: call your friend, the local distributor," I say. "Find out if and when you can get the van."

"And if he says 'no'?"

"Don't let him say 'no'," I say. "You *are* a salesman, and a very good one, so use your skills on your distributor friend. If you're in a clearly labeled delivery vehicle, the discount boys may be confused as to why you're making a cold call to a store that's not even open yet, but at least they won't doubt that you are, in fact, a t-shirt distributor."

"Got it," he says.

"Alright, then go make that call," I say. "The rest of us will head up to my apartment so I can get them hooked into the conferencing app. Meet us up there when you're done."

And, fortunately, I stop myself at the very last second from saying, "You know where it is."

The group, minus Aaron, follows me up out into the street - trying in vain not to look like a parade. We get into my building, and we head up the stairs toward my apartment. I'm in the lead, with the others right behind me. And the higher up we get, the more it occurs to me that I've never had this many people in my apartment at once. I'm bringing all these people - most of whom I barely know - into my world. My small, cozy, safe world.

And that makes me feel… weird. Uneasy. Unsettled.

So I do what I usually do when I feel unsettled: I pretend I'm in an old mystery movie. This time it's that early scene in *The 39 Steps* when the male lead brings the woman to his apartment after the commotion at the mind-reader show, and they walk up that grand old staircase with the railings and marble, and you really feel like they're on an adventure.

My staircase isn't big and it isn't made of marble, but it *is* old. As we head up to my apartment, I really feel like we're living in an old mystery. And if there's one thing I can do, it's old mysteries.

I unlock the front door, and I stand back to let the others go in first. Nelly, who's gotten very familiar with the apartment since she started camping out here yesterday, leads them. She even plays hostess, getting everyone settled with chairs and drinks and directions to the bathroom.

While they do all that, I look out the window. I can see Aaron down in the street, finishing up his phone conversation with the friend who owns the van. Then he clicks his phone off and pumps his fist. Looks like good news.

He double-checks that the discount boys aren't watching him, and then he heads for the door to this building. Nelly buzzes him in.

"Got it!" Aaron says, as soon as he walks into the apartment. "Mike will lend us his van. He's even close by. I'm meeting him at the gas station up Route 5 in twenty minutes. We can have the van to use during his lunch hour, as long as I pay for his lunch at the pizza shop. Small fee for what it's getting us."

"Nice work," I say.

"But are we sure that an hour with the van will be enough time?" Ashley says.

"However this goes - good or bad - it's going to go quick," I say. "That's the only way I see it happening. We're breaking in. We're forcing the issue. Causing a commotion. It's not going to take hours; it's going to take minutes, or less. And that's why we have to plan every step."

I move everything off the coffee table except my laptop and the makeshift map we all drew together down at Yarned.

I hate dismantling my little nook, with my coffee mug and my stack of books and my lap-desk that I've been eating on for pretty much every meal this week. But this is ground zero now.

It's 'go' time.

We get each person hooked up with the conferencing app, to be absolutely sure that they can communicate with me, I can communicate with them, and they can communicate with each other.

I get all their feeds up on my screen at once, arranging each window on my computer in conjunction with the map. I put Ashley's window at the top of my screen, since she and Aaron will be the farthest away from me when they're behind Bank Row, and her phone will be the primary one for both of them. Devin and Nelly's windows go side by side in the middle of the screen, since they'll be next to each other in Dollar Discount and the muffin shop. Finally, Cynthia's window is below and to the left, since she's over here on this side of the street with me.

"Okay, everyone's in," I say. "I can see you all. Now let's test it a little. Everyone go to a different part of the apartment, and we'll see how this works."

I have a very small apartment, but people still manage to put some distance between themselves. Aaron is over in the kitchenette; Devin's in the bathroom; Ashley's in my bedroom; and Cynthia and Nelly are in the opposite two corners here in the living room.

"Okay," I say. "Talk. One by one."

And, of course, even though I asked them to talk one by one, I didn't say who should talk first. So they all say 'hi' pretty much simultaneously, which gets everyone laughing, even Cynthia.

"Let's try that again," I say. "Ashley, you there?"

"I'm here," she says. "Hi everybody."

They all say 'hi' back. It's a little muddled with everyone talking at once, but not too bad.

Okay. Next up. "Aaron?"

"Right here," he says. "Loud and clear."

"Cynthia, is this working for you?"

"I can hear you," Cynthia says. "Can you hear me?"

"Yes, I can. Nelly?"

"Good here, too."

"Devin?" I say. But I don't get a response right away. Hm.

So I repeat, "Devin?"

"Oh, yeah," he says. "I'm here."

"There was a delay there, Devin," I say. "Did you have trouble hearing me a moment ago?"

"No," he says. "It's just that I notice your faucet is leaking, and I was just trying to see if I could tighten it. Sorry - I'm back now."

Once a contractor, always a contractor - I *guess*.

"Alright. Let's all stay focused. Audio is working? Video is working?"

They all agree: Yes, everything is working.

"Good. Now everyone come back in here, and we'll do the big test."

When everyone gets back to me here in the living room, Nelly says, "What's the big test?"

"Movement," I say. "Devin, put your phone on your belt. Yes, like that, the way we talked about. Now walk around."

He does it. He even opens the door of the hall closet to go inside. But before he steps into it, his screen dims.

"Hold on, Devin," I say. "Switch your phone's setting to automatically adjust to lighting changes. You'll be moving around the most of anyone, from the brightness of the sidewalk to the dark of the basement."

He backs out into the light of the hallway, and he adjusts his phone. When he tries it again, I can see what he sees.

"Good. That works," I say. "We're at the last stages of prep now. Let's take a moment to think about what problems could come up, so we can solve them now - before they actually happen. Start by setting your phones to block incoming calls. We don't want anything interrupting us. I'll leave mine on, because if anyone does call me, it will be my sister. She'll be bringing the police with her, *hopefully*, so that's obviously a call we want to take. In fact, speaking of my sister..."

I check my phone again for messages from Fi. No new text, no voicemail, no missed calls. I check my work email and my personal email. Nothing there either.

Nelly checks all her accounts for anything from Wanda. Same result.

"Okay, then. That's it," I say. "We've done everything here, so go to your stations and we'll do a final check."

Everyone leaves - except for Devin. He holds back, to give everyone else time to get into position before he sets things in motion. Except he's doing more than holding back: he's... *lingering.*

Hm.

"Hey," I say. "You're smiling. Why?"

"I'm smiling at this whole plan you came up with," he says.

"You think it's crazy," I say. "You think it's stupid."

"Just the opposite, Lizzie. I'm impressed. It's a good plan. Is it from some old movie or something?"

"Kind of, actually. I borrowed bits and pieces from a bunch of them. But... how did you know I like old movies?"

"Just a feeling," he says. "Plus, in old movies - at least the ones I've seen - often little things mean a lot. You're good at noticing little things."

"Wow. Thank you," I say. And there's something else I want to talk to him about. But at the moment, with him just casually leaning against the easy chair, smiling at me, I can't think of what it is.

Oh, right: freeing Wanda from captivity. And stopping bank robbers. That's what I want to talk to him about.

Obviously.

Focus, Lizzie. Focus.

"So... to be clear, you're really okay with what we're about to do here?" I say. "You're okay with the plan - and your specific role in it? Your part is the most dangerous at first. It wasn't very fair of me to ask you about it in front of everyone. You might have felt pressure from the others to say 'yes.'"

"The plan is good," he says. "In its own crazy way it makes total sense. And all I have to do is get through a door. I'm a contractor; I can get through doors. It's nice when your skills actually get put to good use."

I have a warm feeling inside as he says this, and I think back to that moment twelve years ago, when I was tutoring him in eleventh grade on that crazy word problem with the rolling cup.

And I remember that, on that day, he failed to solve that abstract, theoretical problem. But how many *actual* problems has he solved since then - every day, working with levels and measurements and weights and levers?

Tons of them.

So he's right: this will be a breeze for him. He's here, he's relaxed, and he's ready.

"Well, you're certainly taking this all in stride," I say.

"It helps to know the others will be nearby. And..."

"And...?"

"You'll be here," he says, "watching over us the whole time. Making sure the movie ends the right way."

He's looking at me. And his eyes are blue. Like, really blue. And they seem to be getting even bluer, somehow, the longer we stand here.

And I hear soft music playing in the background. Violins.

Not really, of course. I don't actually hear anything except the sounds from the conferencing app on my laptop, as everyone else gets into position.

But, wow, I really need to improve my timing, because yesterday, at a completely inconvenient time on the street, Devin and I almost had a moment. And now, at an even more inconvenient time, we definitely have a moment.

Really, Lizzie. You need to snap out of this. Back to the matter at hand.

"Go," I say to Devin. "Get out of here before we... Well, just get out and go down to your starting position."

He leaves, but not without adding one more smile. And one more shade of blue to his eyes.

And then I'm finally interrupted - thank you - by an incoming message from Ashley on the conference app. They're picking up the truck. So far, so good - at least until her window in the app goes black.

What? A problem?

So I text her: *Your screen is blank. What's up?*

I get a response from her very quickly: *No problem. A surprise.*

A surprise? What does that mean? Must be a typo from auto-correct. I *hope* it's a typo from auto-correct, because surprises are not what we need right now.

Then, after a moment, I get another text from her: *We have the truck - we're driving back towards Teabridge. Be there in six minutes.*

Whatever the surprise is, things still seem to be progressing. So I look down through the window at the muffin shop. I see a customer stroll up to the door. He reads the 'closed' sign Nelly put up there, and then he casually moves on. Good. I'm glad that customers aren't making a big deal about the place being closed again. It probably helps that the lights are all off inside the shop, so they can't see Nelly hiding in the shadows. I know for sure she's in the shadows because her feed on the conferencing app is the darkest. It's got a cool mystery look to it; you see just enough to wonder what exactly it is that you're seeing. A woman hiding in those shadows? Spying on her neighbors? No - it couldn't be.

Yes. It is.

"Nelly, you look ready," I whisper. "Are you?"

Instead of answering me verbally, she takes her phone and moves it up and down, which makes her feed look like it's nodding. I have to cover my mouth to keep from laughing too loud and blowing her cover.

I give her a thumbs up, and then I turn my attention back to Devin. He got down the stairs quickly, and I now see him striding across the street. He checks the hinges to the door of the discount store. Then he pulls his generator out of his van and puts it on the sidewalk, right in front of Dollar Discount. He returns to the back of his van, and he loads up his tool belt.

He looks into his phone: "Final check-in from me," he says. "I'm set for tools. All I need to do is turn on the generator and then start my break-in work."

"Good," I say. "Let's double-check the phone app."

He puts the phone back in the slot on his belt where he had it before. Then he turns around slowly, to show me a moving image again. So now I'm looking two places at once: down at the street, seeing him turn around, and then at the conference app on my laptop here on the coffee table, seeing the shaky image of the buildings that spin through his camera's view. It's especially funny when I see the front of Yarned pass through his feed in the app-window, and then I look in Cynthia's feed, and I see Devin. It's like two parallel worlds have somehow intersected.

Actually it's more than just funny. It's nice to see how quickly we've all become connected as a group.

Time for final adjustments.

"Cynthia," I say. "Can you hear me?"

"I hear you."

"Rotate your phone a little to your left. I need a better view of the alley."

"Got it."

She rotates it.

"Perfect," I say. "This will be the primary camera position for you. Let's call it 'Position A.' 'Position B' will be where you just had it. And you should keep a physical eye on the Dollar Discount storefront the whole time. You can see deeper into it than I can."

"Excellent," she says. "I'll do that."

Ashley's feed finally pops back up on my laptop, thankfully, and I see the blurry images of the streets they pass as they drive back here towards Cottage Street from the gas station where they picked up the van. And once my eyes adjust to the blur of her screen, I actually begin to distinguish the buildings. That orange blur is the supermarket. That rosy-silver blur is the physical therapy building next to it - all red brick and big shiny windows.

"Are you passing Dwight Street?" I say, just to be sure I know what I'm seeing.

"Yes, we are," Ashley says. "And we're ready to show you the surprise."

She turns the phone on Aaron, and he's wearing a dark blue work-shirt with the name 'Mike" stenciled above the front pocket. It's an actual delivery man's shirt.

"Cool, right?" Ashley says. "And you'll never guess what else?"

"Don't tell me," I say. "You, too?"

She turns the phone around to show me that yes, she is also wearing the same dark blue work shirt - though hers says 'Jerome.'

"It's like you told us before," she says. "Anything that will get them to believe that we're legit delivery people will buy us those few seconds we need. And we were super quick about putting them on. We didn't delay - I promise."

"It's okay," I say. "You're doing great. Except I hate to ask you this, but can you dial down the jewelry? You're posing as someone who works with their hands doing physical labor. So take off anything that dangles or would get damaged if you were hauling heavy boxes all day. Same thing with Aaron, actually."

"You mean his bling, as he calls it?"

She means his platinum watch. And, trust me, I advised him on many occasions not to call it his 'bling.'

"Yes," I say. "Tell him to take it off. And while you're at it, is there anything you can do about your make-up? You look great - don't get me wrong. But that's kind of the problem. I just can't picture a first-shift delivery woman taking the time to do a smoky eye at five in the morning. Maybe after work, she would. But not before."

"Oh, okay. I see what you mean."

She's so relaxed and kind as she says this, just rolling with it. I'm surprised at how good she is to work with. She has her quirks, but she listens and takes in what I'm saying.

"Thanks, Ash," I say. "Where are you guys now?"

"Hm. I don't know." She turns the camera back to the street, and I recognize it. They're still a few miles away, but there are no more traffic lights, and their arrival is imminent.

"Alright everyone," I say into the conferencing app. "We're looking at about four minutes until 'go time.' Four minutes."

I get nods and 'sounds goods' all around.

"Nelly, just to confirm," I say. "The discount boys are in their store now?"

"In the store or in the basement. I can't tell for sure," she whispers.

"But they haven't gone out? They're still around?"

"I've had an eye on their old van the whole time. It hasn't gone anywhere."

"Alright, so our plan still moves forward," I say. "Devin you're still ready with your tools?"

"More than ready."

"And the generator is ready and full of gas?"

"All set with the generator."

"Okay. Then pull your van up to the alley, and block it from the street side."

"Will do."

"Everyone else, do any last things you need to do," I say. "And then hold in the 'ready' position."

Okay, now that everyone is all set, I realize that I have these last few minutes to do my own final preparations as well.

And what do I need?

I need to settle myself, so that I'm in the best possible frame of mind to direct this complicated and vital operation from here on out.

And I do have an idea of how I want to settle myself?

Yes, I do have an idea. Should I do it, though?

I *want* to do it. So hey - why not?

I go into my bedroom to change into my pajamas.

Yes. My pajamas.

Why not? Devin fixed up his toolbelt, Nelly dressed all dark, and Ashley and Aaron changed into those uniforms. They all got into their parts in their own ways, and the best way for me to get into my part is to dress the way that makes me feel most powerful. Most centered.

Most 'me.'

I open my dresser drawer to reveal... wait for it... my purple wisteria flannels, neatly folded and ready for me to wear.

I'd forgotten that I'd laundered them along with Nelly's jeans, and now it's like they've magically appeared in my drawer like a sign from the Universe that says, "Yes. Put these on."

And one thing I know for sure about myself: I can put on pajamas quickly. Taking them off can sometimes take ages, especially on a cold winter's morning when I really want to stay inside all day. But putting them on? Well, they're already on.

I'm back at Ground Zero.

And it's 'go time.'

The Operation

Well, not *quite* go-time, it turns out, because I see in the top feed on my laptop screen that Ashley is using her phone like a mirror as she ties her highlighted ringlets into a ponytail. She's got an 'I think I actually like this look' expression on her face.

"Ashley, that's enough adjustments," I say. "You look fine. We need you on task now."

"Sorry!" she says. "I'm back. And this is your street, isn't it?"

She turns her screen back to the forward-facing camera. The curve to Bank Row is just three blocks away.

"Alright, our undercover delivery van is approaching," I say to the group. "Everyone stay ready."

As Ashley and Aaron approach the alley next to the financial advisors, they slow down and put on their blinker, preparing to turn into that alley - which is *not* the turn they want.

I knew it would be an easy mistake to make, which is why I went over it with the map. Still, it's happened anyway. But I suppose the good news is that this minor almost-glitch gives us a chance to work through making adjustments on the fly. Better to practice now than when things really heat up - very soon.

"Ashley, no," I say. "Not into that alley. Tell Aaron to keep going, and I'll guide you. Aaron, are you hearing this?"

I hear Aaron's voice, fainter than Ashley's. "Hearing it!"

I guide them down the far end of Bank Row, past the Tile and Flooring shop.

"Okay, slow up - slower - do you see it?"

"Just a small path," Ashley says.

"That's it. You're right, it's small," I say. "But you can get through it. Just go slowly."

"You sure?" Ashley aims her phone right at it.

"Yes, go." They go.

Then I see their window on my screen become dimmer, as they pass through the darker shadows of this far entrance.

I see from Cynthia's feed that all is quiet in the alley. Devin is just waiting in front of the discount store, tools in hand. Nelly is still hiding in the rear hallway of the muffin shop, waiting to see Ashley and Aaron's van appear in the rear lot.

As I glance from feed to feed in the different windows of my computer screen, I start to get the hang of it. And it all becomes one story, just with shifting camera angles.

Ashley and Aaron finally do emerge into the rear lot. They park at a skewed angle - the way someone rushing to make a quick delivery might do - blocking the entrance they just came through. Good.

They wait there in the van for a minute. I wait up here in my apartment. Everyone else waits where they are. Nothing happens. The guys don't come out of the discount store.

"Should I go knock on the door or something?" Aaron says.

I don't want to say 'yes,' because this wasn't in the plan. But everyone is in position. If this is going to happen, we'll just have to make it happen.

"Okay, go ahead," I say. "But stay outside. Don't go in the store, even if they ask you to. Draw them out instead."

"Should I go, too?" Ashley says.

"No - just Aaron. You stay with your phone just where you are, filming the whole thing."

"I can handle going with him, you know," she says. "You don't have to protect me."

"I know you can handle it," I say, "and I'm not protecting you. I mean, I *am* protecting you - but I'm trying to protect everyone. And from where I'm sitting up here, the best way to do that is to have a complete picture. Please, stay where you are. And can you hold the phone outside your window so I can hear what they're saying?"

She sticks her phone out, hiding it by tucking it behind the side view mirror.

"Nice," I say. "Okay, Aaron. Go."

He gets out of the van, and he walks toward the rear door of the discount store. I switch my attention to Nelly's feed as he approaches the building, and I can see the eager look on his face. I want to tell him to ease up, relax. But he can't hear me right now, so I just have to wait to see how this all turns out.

He knocks on the rear door.

He waits a minute.

Nothing.

I check all the feeds. No action anywhere.

The wait feels endless.

And...

Finally I see faint movement at the discount store's back door. And then it opens.

Cory is there. And even from this distance, through the lens of an obstructed cell phone camera, he looks tough. Suspicious. And smart.

"Yeah, hi," Aaron says to him. "I've got a delivery for... this is a discount store, yeah? Dollar Discount of Teabridge?"

"We're not taking deliveries," Cory says, flatly. And then he calls out, "Griff?"

"But it's a discount store, isn't it?" Aaron says, trying to keep Cory's attention. "At least tell me I have that right?"

"Yeah it's a -"

"And this is Teabridge Village, so... I gotta figure the delivery is going to you."

"Whatever you're selling, we don't want it," Cory says. "Move along."

"I'm not selling; I'm delivering. Are you sure you don't want to get your boss out here?"

"He's not my boss," Cory says, "And this is not the time."

"I don't mean to bother you, pal," Aaron says. "Can you just step out here? Let me show you what I've got here. It won't take long. I promise."

It's a key moment. Aaron is taking a risk. Will Cory come

out?

Aaron waits for one second, then two seconds. Then he does something subtle but very effective: he shrugs as if to say, *No big deal. Just come out for a moment. Why not?*

And boy is Aaron a good salesman, because it works. Cory does come out. Aaron told me once that it's the little touches that do it - syncing your gestures with the other person's rhythms, and then subtly guiding them your way. Cory was caught off-guard by the shrug just now, and he just kind of found himself stepping outside.

"Thanks, pal," Aaron says, showing him the clipboard. "I have it written down here that your partner - or whoever he is - he ordered these t-shirts I've got in the back of my van. So I'm just saying, if he ordered them, you don't want to be turning them away, especially since we won't be back this month. I mean, you've got a store to open, right?"

"We didn't order these."

"Can I just talk to him? This guy Griff, or whatever his name is?"

Cory rolls his eyes. He's frustrated at Aaron, the situation, and most especially with himself for the thing he's about to do, which is to relent to Aaron's persuasion.

"Griff!" he says, and he doesn't call it this time. He yells it. "Griff, get out here!"

Cory turns back to Aaron and stares hard at him until finally, ten seconds later, Griff emerges. He pauses at the door, quite happy to let Cory deal with whatever the problem is.

But Cory is having none of that. He gives Griff a dirty look. Really dirty. "Get out here," he says.

There's a pause here. A hard pause. A stand-off, even between Griff and Cory. And that's risky for us. So, on impulse, I say, "Devin, turn on your generator, and get ready."

Devin switches it on, and it roars to life so irritatingly that it kind of pushes Griff out the back door, and I see him stumble begrudgingly into the parking lot.

Good. That's two of them. I'd love to have all three of the

discount boys accounted for, and the only one who's not outside yet is Nate. Unless they sent him home after making him stay up all night (which I doubt, given how poorly they treat him) he's still inside somewhere.

But we have to move at some point, and that means taking the risk that we'll be able to deal with Nate when we come to him.

So I make the call: "Devin - go!"

Devin takes his pry bar and gets to work on the door.

"Cynthia, focus in on Devin," I say. "Real close."

Cynthia moves her camera, and I see Devin gently wedging his pry bar into the space between the door and the frame.

"No time for craftsmanship, Devin," I say. "Bust through the door as quick as you can."

He takes his hammer off his belt and gives the pry-bar a whack. "Could you hear that?" he says.

"Barely," I say. "The generator is blocking out the noise, so just go for it."

Devin gets to pounding, so I turn my attention back to the rear-lot feed, to see how Aaron is doing. He's now stepped closer to Griff - a confidence-inspiring sales tactic that says, 'We're just friends here. No need to be separate on this thing.'

But Cory is shaking his head. He's not buying it. And any moment now, he's going to kick Aaron out.

So I look again at Devin, but he's really only slightly more aggressive than he was a minute ago.

"Devin," I say. "Listen, Sweetheart. You need to get in there now, whatever it takes. We've got, like, seconds remaining here."

And just to be clear, I meant 'Sweetheart' the way you'd say, 'buddy,' or 'dude.' Because he isn't my sweetheart, obviously. I mean, I know that sometimes when two people go through a difficult situation together - like, I don't know, breaking into a discount store to rescue a muffin baker - it can bring them so close that they fall in love. I hope that Devin doesn't think that's what's happening here, though from the inspired way he is now completely attacking the front door, he probably does.

He bangs the pry bar into the lower right hand corner of the door, just above the hinges, and then he yanks back, ripping the screws right out. Then he hops up on the ladder and does the same thing with the top hinge - which comes out even quicker, having been loosened when he did the first one.

And that's it: the door falls toward him.

"Be careful Devin!" I shout, and fortunately he grabs the door by the wooden edges, preventing the big glass part from falling right into his face.

I glance at the rear parking lot feed to see if the discount boys heard these new noises, and sure enough, Cory isn't looking at Aaron anymore; he's looking off in the distance in a 'Did I just hear something?' kind of way.

"Ashley," I say. "Cory thinks he heard Devin. Get his attention. Distract him. Stall him."

So Ashley finally does get out, which at this point is a nice move, because Cory was about to leave the scene completely to investigate the noise.

"Don't tell me we have another order problem?" she says - loud, and impossible to ignore. She's walking toward the others, pretending to walk-and-text, but actually keeping the camera aimed at them the whole time.

"Mike, if I told you once, I told you a hundred million thousand billion times," she says. "When you take an order, you have to rectify the restock code!"

'Rectify the restock code' is total gibberish, of course, and it cracks me up that she says it in such a ridiculously self-important way. Yet it's working - somehow - so I focus back on Devin, who's now through the door and into the Dollar Discount showroom. The deeper he goes, the darker it gets, until he's all the way in a back hallway that looks just like the one in Wanda's shop.

"That's the door to the basement!" I whisper. "It's gotta be.

Go!"

Devin opens the basement door and starts to walk down.
He takes a pen-light from his toolbelt and clicks it on. Perfect.
It gives us enough light to see, but not so much that the guys
out back will notice.

The area at the bottom of the stairs is just as confusing as it
is in Wanda's basement: a tight turn, and then a door, and
then another tight turn back in the other direction. And then
there's a long hallway - again, just like in Wanda's basement.

And this one leads down to... a cramped storage room full
of office equipment, a rusty metal filing cabinet, an old office
chair with cushions eaten away by mice, and an easel for a
business presentation.

What? Huh?

I've seen this all before.

I open my mouth to speak to Devin, but it's really hard to
get words out because what I have to say makes no sense at
all.

"Devin..." I say. "You're in Wanda's basement!"

He takes his phone out of his belt and looks at the screen,
to see my face.

"What are you talking about?"

"I don't know!" I say. "I don't get it! But I'm telling you,
Nelly and I went into Wanda's basement earlier to look for
her, and we found a room just like that!"

"So the two adjoining basements mirror each other," he
says. "That makes sense. It's for a builder to configure them
the same way like this."

"No!" I say. "I'm not saying their basement is *like* Wanda's
basement. I'm saying you're *in* Wanda's basement right now.
Look at the filing cabinet. Is the bottom drawer pulled out?"

"Well, it's just kind of..."

"Collapsed?" I say.

"Yeah."

This is crazy. This is so crazy. I mean, unless he stepped
through a vortex or something, there's gotta be an

explanation. I mean, how did he get into Wanda's basement?

Devin has stopped moving. He's just standing there. I can see that his penlight is tilted up toward the ceiling, but what's he looking for up there?

"Devin!" I shout-whisper into my computer's microphone. "Hey, Devin! What are you doing?"

"This is starting to make sense," he says. "Do you notice the direction of the beams? Normally, joists go the shorter way, eave-to-eave - which in this building is front-to-rear. But these go the long way, from gable-to-gable."

"What are you saying, Devin? Can you just tell me in non-carpenter talk?

"I am standing in the storage area for the discount store," he says. "But I'm not underneath the discount store. I'm underneath Wanda's shop. And that means..."

"Wanda shares the basement with Dollar Discount!" I scream.

The two shops each have their own separate stairways, but they lead to the very same place - somehow joining at the bottom. The two basements look like the same place because they *are* the same place!

I look at Nelly's feed to tell her this.

But she's gone. Her feed is all dark and blurry. And that tells me she heard everything we just said. And as soon as she realized Wanda was in her basement, she ran down to try to rescue her. I totally respect her for doing that, of course. But at the same time...

"Nelly, be careful!" I say, though I have no idea whether she can hear me at this point. For eight endless seconds, I see nothing but darkness in her feed, until finally I see her show up in Devin's feed, running towards him.

"Over there!" she says to him, and she points to the old door that we never checked when we came down here yesterday, because it just looked dusty and it had a board nailed across it. Now it has a bunch of boards across it, from floor to ceiling.

"She must be in there," Nelly says. "It's the only place we didn't look."

Devin goes over and examines the door.

"The discount boys put those boards up, didn't they?" she asks him.

"It certainly looks that way," Devin says. "Look at the nail heads. They're new. This hasn't been boarded up for very long, I can tell you that."

He's already got his pry-bar out. And any careful craftsmanship is long gone, as he rips the first board off in two very hard pulls.

While he gets to work, I look to Ashley's feed and I see… no one. Just the back of the building. No discount boys, and no Aaron.

"Ashley, what's going on?"

"They went inside!" Ashley says. "Aaron is following them!"

"Devin! Nelly! Did you hear that?" I shout. "They're coming down! They're heading your way!"

Devin tosses the pry-bar to Nelly, and she picks up where he left off, pulling the boards off the door, while he brings the boards he's already pulled off over to the door to the Dollar Discount stairway.

He slams that door shut, just at the moment I hear the thumping of the discount boys coming down the stairs.

Before they can push their way through it, Devin's nailed up one of the boards to block them out. The door shakes as they start running into it with their shoulders, trying to bust their way through. So Devin nails up another board, just as the first one starts to come loose.

I hear more thumping and some kind of scuffle. Aaron must have caught up with them, and - ugh - I just know he's trying to fight them both at the same time.

So Nelly - please hurry with the old door.

She rips off the next two boards quickly, but the one at the bottom is the stickiest. So Devin leaves the door with the discount boys behind it, and he joins her, grabbing a metal strip from a broken old shelf on the floor, and he wedges it into the bottom board, right next to where Nelly has the pry bar. Together they pull harder and harder until, yes! It comes off.

They get through the door and into another storage room. Along the side walls are filled with baking equipment - pans and bowls and sacks of flour. Along the rear wall sits a deep freezer.

In the middle of all this, in the center of the room, sits two plastic water jugs, a loaf of bread, and two chairs.

And in those chairs sit… wait for it... Nate and Wanda.

Wanda's alive - and apparently well.

Wow.

Nelly runs over and gives her a big hug.

I wait a moment to let them have their reunion, but I can't wait two moments.

"Nelly, get out of there!" I shout. "You and Devin - get Wanda, and get out of there!"

"I will," Nelly says. "Auntie Wanda, are you okay? Can you walk out of here?"

"I can *run* out of here," Wanda says. But first she turns to Nate.

"Listen, Sweetheart. Stay down here - like we talked about," she says. "Hide in the closet or something until the police come, and I'll take care of this. I'll tell them everything, just like we talked about. Do you understand?"

"I do," he says. "And… thank you."

Finally, they're ready to come out. So I check the other feeds, to make sure the coast is clear.

I hear lots of thumping from… somewhere. Then I look at Ashley's feed, and I see the discount boys burst back up through the rear door into the parking lot. They must have figured out that Wanda's been freed, and now they're making a run for it.

They hop into the rusty old van, which awkwardly leaps

forward when Cory roars up the engine and slams into drive. He tears around the corner into the alley but then screeches to a stop halfway down when he sees Devin's van blocking the street. He slams into reverse and hits the gas too hard. The vehicle lurches backward at an angle, crashing into the brick sidewall of Bank Row. So they leap out of the van and run back down the alley, to escape out through the rear parking lot somehow.

Except there, at the end of the alley, is a genuinely fearsome sight: Ashley. She's five foot three and a hundred and ten pounds at the most. Yet what stops them, besides the supremely confident look on her face, is that she's holding a tire iron like a baseball bat - reminding me of that company softball game when the outfielders severely underestimated her ability to swing a blunt object.

After all the bad decisions Griff and Cory have made in the last week, they finally make a good one: they turn around and run away, squeezing past the smashed van and then finally bursting out onto the street to yet another fearsome sight: a seventy-two year old woman brandishing a knitting needle. It's Cynthia, standing right in the middle of the street, blocking their right turn down Cottage Street - somehow looking just as formidable as Ashley does.

So they take a left turn, stopping short a third and final time at the sight of the flashing blue lights of Julia Ramos' cruiser.

"Sir, I need you to stop right there," Officer Ramos says over her speaker.

They freeze. They look back at Cynthia who's now been joined by Devin, with a ball-peen hammer in one hand and claw hammer in the other. And Ashley has emerged from the alley, joined by Nelly and Wanda. And if that's not enough, Aaron staggers up behind them. His usually perfect hair is messed up, and he's got the beginning of a shiner from the scuffle he just had with the discount boys. But he's still standing strong and ready for another round.

Officer Ramos gets out of the cruiser.

And - uh-oh - the person who gets out of the passenger side is… Fiona.

I better get down there.

I close up the laptop and run out of the apartment as fast as my slippers will allow me, and I fly down the stairs and out the front door to the street, as two more cruisers arrive.

Griff makes a futile, last-ditch effort to talk his way out of the situation. "Officer, this isn't how it looks," he says.

Julia Ramos glances over at Wanda, who - despite her eternally positive attitude - still has the ragged look of someone who just emerged from three days and nights trapped in a boarded-up basement room.

Ramos turns back to Griff and smirks at him. "Sir," she says. "*Really* now."

So is *that* where Fi got that phrase?

Speaking of Fi, I prepare myself for the scolding that I assume is coming my way.

But before she can say anything, Nelly shouts, "Lizzie!"

And I guess this is the first time that she - or anyone else - has noticed that I've come down here to the street, because they all turn to me.

"That was awesome, Lizzie!" Ashley says.

"Totally awesome, boss!" Aaron says.

"You did it, Lizzie!" Devin says.

"*We* did it," I say. "All of us."

Then I look at Fi with a 'please don't be mad' half-cringe.

She rolls her eyes and shakes her head. After all, how could she be mad at a girl wearing panda slippers?

The other officers join the scene, and they load Griff and Cory into one of the cruisers.

Then Officer Ramos approaches Wanda. "I'm going to drive you to the hospital," she says. "I understand that you'd probably rather stay here with your niece. But we err on the side of caution in cases like this. Plus, I'm going to need a witness statement from you."

"I understand," Wanda says. "But I should tell you something first: there's one more guy. A younger one. Nate. He was helping them all week, *reluctantly*, until they locked him in the basement room with me this morning. He's down there now, hiding in the closet. He promised me he won't make trouble when you go there."

Ramos nods to two of the other officers, and they go into the discount store to retrieve Nate.

"Before they return with him, I want to say something," Wanda tells Ramos.

"Go ahead, Ma'am."

"If you haven't guessed by the tone of my voice, I have some sympathy for this Nate boy. Because if it wasn't for him, I'd still be locked in their basement, on my way to an even worse fate."

"I can vouch for that," Nelly says.

"Thank you," Wanda says. "And to be clear, I'm not asking you to let him off the hook. He's done wrong, and he knows it. But he's not like the others. And he'll help you if he can."

Ramos nods. "Help is good," she says. "And there's plenty of time to sort through all of that."

"Auntie Wanda, do you want me to come with you?" Nelly says.

"Of course I do," Wanda says. "But I'm fine. Really. And you need to get a good night's sleep, since you'll be getting up early to open the shop. Miss Groff here likes her muffin by five forty-five."

Nelly laughs. "So I've learned," she says. "Alright, I'll stay here. But I'll have my phone on at all times, and I'll check it every five minutes. If you need anything, just let me know."

"I will," Wanda says. "And do you need the keys to my house?"

"At some point," Nelly says. "But for tonight, at least until you get back, I think I'll just..."

Nelly looks at me with a question in her eyes.

"Stay at my place?" I say. "Absolutely."

"What a kind and generous attitude," Wanda says.

"I learned it from you," I say.

When Nelly walks her aunt over to the cruiser, I turn to the others.

Cynthia is re-opening Yarned for the Happy Hour Knitting Club, which is already gathering on the street outside. Something tells me they're going to have plenty to chat about tonight.

Devin, Ashley, and Aaron are close by, talking animatedly as they recap the crazy adventure we just shared. They're getting along. Laughing. Finishing each other's sentences.

And a part of me thinks that I better break this up as soon as possible, because if I don't, then the next thing I know, Aaron will be setting up a double-date for next week: him and Ashley, and me and Devin. And probably trying to set up Nelly while he's at it.

And that's just totally a bad idea.

Right? I mean… right?

I mean… am I really thinking of going out with my ex-boyfriend, who's been totally nice to me the whole time we've been broken up, and his new girlfriend, who totally came through in this tense and dangerous situation, exceeding everyone's expectations yet again?

Well, yes. I *am* thinking that.

But that's for next week, because tonight I already have plans: an old movie with a new friend.

Nelly returns from helping out her aunt. "Do you want to hear something funny, but also kind of spooky?" she says.

"Good spooky or bad spooky?" I say.

"Good spooky," she says. "When Nate and Wanda were trapped down there together, he told her the whole story of what Griff and Corey were doing all week, and it turns out they were trying - unsuccessfully - to dig a tunnel into the basement of the bank. Wanda found out about it when she was gathering supplies down there. So they kidnapped her and made Nate guard her overnight."

"Wait a second," I say. "Are you telling me… that we were exactly right?"

"That's what I'm telling you," she says.

"Wow," I say. "That *is* spooky. In fact, of all the strange and spooky things that happened this week, this might very well be the strangest and spookiest."

Nelly nods in a big way.

So I figure this is as good a time as any to turn to the person I've somehow avoided up to now: my sister.

"Fi, you're smiling," I say. "Does that mean you're not mad that I didn't wait for you?"

"It's pretty hard to be mad at someone who just rescued a woman from being kidnapped - and foiled a bank robbery in the process," she says. "I couldn't be prouder. So go ahead - you and Nelly should go have your slumber party tonight. You deserve it."

"Thank you, Sis," I say. "But you say that like you're not coming, too. Please tell me you're coming, too."

"Oh, totally!" Nelly says. "You should totally come! And Lizzie will lend you some pajamas. She has, like, a ton of them, you know."

"So I've heard," Fi says. "And thank you for the offer. But the only way I could say 'yes' is if I brought the girls, too."

"Are you actually asking if two girls aged five and seven are welcome at a pajama party?" I say. "Because the answer is yes. Totally yes."

It's the Pajama Club, after all.

Everyone is welcome.

Also by Maizie Waters:

Gifts from Afar: a Teabridge Romance

And the upcoming Murder Most Foul: a Night School Mystery